REFORMING HUNT

Cover design by T.E. Black Designs

REFORMING HUNT

USA TODAY BESTSELLING AUTHOR
JULES BARNARD

FRESH FICTION PUBLISHING
JULESBARNARDBOOKS.COM

CHAPTER ONE

Hunt Cade breathed in the scent of booze and perfume and let out a contented sigh. He was in his element inside the club at Blue Casino. He flagged the bartender, who lifted his chin in acknowledgment. Within a minute, Hunt's favorite drink would be delivered to him.

Hunt's brother Adam stood across the room, talking to a coworker. Adam, the traitor, worked at Blue Casino, while Hunt and their other three brothers had been holding down the fort at Club Tahoe since their father's passing.

Three, four years? Had it been that long since Ethan Cade died? It seemed like only yesterday that Hunt stood outside his dad's hospital room and learned the news. And it hadn't been a quick death. Their father had been diagnosed with cancer months earlier, but he'd suffered in silence. By the time Hunt and his brothers discovered the truth, their father was gone.

Adam finally looked up from his conversation and met Hunt's gaze. He murmured something to the coworker and weaved his way over, looking slick in his customary designer suit.

"I'm grabbing a beer," Hunt's buddy Chris said. He was Hunt's wingman tonight. Chris took off for the bar, a swagger in his step as he flashed a grin at a passing blonde.

Adam walked up and clapped Hunt on the shoulder. "Weren't you here last night?"

Hunt scanned the room. "Your point?"

"You need a life."

Hunt coughed into the palm of his hand. "*I* need a life? You're married, and appear to have forgotten there's an entire world outside."

Adam grinned lewdly. "Because it's more fun inside."

Point taken. Adam's wife Hayden was beautiful. No doubt his brother found ways to occupy their time. But still, where was the variety? Where was the energy that vibrated with the hunt? No pun intended.

Adam eyed him. "You might consider something longer than a one-night stand."

"I'll stick with my current entertainments, thank you very much." Hunt had already scouted the place, but he made a show of scanning the room again to prove to his brother that his words didn't affect him.

Sadly, Hunt saw familiar faces, which only proved Adam's point.

Out of all the Cade sons, Hunt had gotten around the most. Was that so wrong?

Adam shoved his hand in his pants pocket, looking annoyingly concerned. "Try not to contract a venereal disease."

Hunt glared. "It's called a *condom.* I'm as clean as spring rain." He straightened his button-down shirt, still wearing jeans. No way he'd be caught in the monkey suits Adam donned each day.

"Are you sure about that?"

"Yes, I'm sure," Hunt said. "I go to the doctor, you asshole." Damn, his brothers were annoying.

Adam glanced at his Rolex. "Just checking." But Hunt could tell his "activities" these last few years worried his brother. Never used to. It wasn't until recently, when all of his brothers had settled down, that Hunt received more heat than normal from his family.

"I'm off," Adam said. "Hayden and I have plans."

Hunt narrowed his eyes. "Real plans? Or are you just saying that to take off and get your wife into bed?"

Adam shook his head slowly as though Hunt was being ridiculous.

Such a hypocrite. Adam presented a polished exterior, but Hunt knew better. His brother had his own history with beautiful women. That part of his life might be behind him, but Adam didn't even hide the fact that he took advantage of the best perk of being married. As far as Hunt was concerned, it was the *only* perk.

"I don't seduce my wife every minute of the day," Adam said. "Levi and Emily are coming over for dinner, and then we're watching *The Bachelor*."

Hunt closed his eyes and sighed heavily. "Hanging out with our older brother and his girlfriend and watching reality TV is not 'real plans.' You might as well pull on an adult diaper and sign up for Life Alert. You've got one foot in the grave, my man."

Adam waved goodbye to the coworker he'd been talking to earlier. "Don't knock it until you try it."

"I'll pass," Hunt said distractedly, in desperate need of kicking off the night. His brothers' love lives were depressing.

"I'll see you at the next beer night?" Adam said. "Or

maybe I'll see you here tomorrow?" He quirked his eyebrow.

Likely, Hunt thought. "Beer night is always a go, and make sure you bring Hayden this time. That woman works too much."

"Tell me about it." Adam shook Hunt's hand and took off.

A few minutes later, Hunt leaned against plush gray cushions inside the lounge filled to the brim with beautiful vacationers and the fashionable elite of Lake Tahoe. Chris had found them an optimal location—perfect for viewing the bar and dance floor. Hunt sipped his gin and tonic, relaxing for the first time all day.

"Bar. Four o'clock," Chris said, and gulped his beer.

Hunt glanced in the direction his friend indicated, though "friend" might be a strong word for the partnership he and Chris had formed.

Chris worked at Club Tahoe as a doorman, and he was always up for going out. Though Hunt suspected it had something to do with the comps Hunt's connections afforded them all over town. But their wingman partnership was mutually beneficial. It was easier to approach women in pairs. And as Hunt got older, most of his friends had dropped off to be in relationships.

More fools them.

Hunt had already noticed the two women sitting at the bar. "Which one?"

One of the women wore a short metallic dress and five-inch heels. She had long, dark hair and heavy makeup, and she looked like an Instagram model. The woman next to her, however, was a bit of an oddball in this environment. She wore fitted jeans and a sexy top, which both worked. What threw him were the shoes. She had on those rubber shoes nurses wore. Glogs? Clogs? It was a strange choice for a high-end club.

"The sexy one," Chris said.

Hunt scanned both women. Their styles were different, but they were both pretty. Clog woman simply had a more natural look. Then again, Hunt could find something beautiful in any woman.

"I'm game." Hunt picked up his drink and they strode over.

Clog woman caught sight of them first. She ducked her head and whispered something to her friend.

"Having a good evening, ladies?" Chris said to the dark-haired woman.

Not exactly original, Hunt thought, but in a place like this, people weren't looking for poetry. They were looking for a hookup.

"We are, actually." The dark-haired woman nudged her friend, and the other woman murmured something that sounded like a choked assent.

Now that Hunt was up close, he caught the golden highlights in clog woman's long, wavy, light brown hair. Pretty hair that fell in waves and looked soft to the touch. He hadn't gotten a good look at her eyes yet, but her full, pillowy mouth was definitely kissable.

She swiped the side of a chilled glass of beer and avoided his gaze.

It could be shyness, but Hunt had been around long enough to detect the signs of someone who wasn't here to be social. Which always confused the hell out of him. Why go to a club if you weren't interested in socializing?

Rarely did Hunt run into a woman who wasn't interested in talking—or more—but when he did, he walked away. He was here for mutual flirtation.

Leave it to Chris to target a pair of women with one-half not interested.

The last thing Hunt wanted was to make the woman uncomfortable. Still, he had to try talking to her for Chris's sake. It was a part of his wingman duties.

Chris chatted with the Instagram model lookalike, and Hunt turned to her friend. "I'm Hunt. What's your name?"

She set her beer down and shook his outstretched hand. "Abby."

Soft hands and a pretty voice. "You come here often?" She didn't. He'd know, because he was here almost every night.

"Not at all."

"Are you from out of town?" he asked. She was a conundrum inside this place.

"I live here," she said. "I just don't get out much."

"That's a shame," he said, adding a flirtatious depth to his tone.

She finally looked up, long enough that he glimpsed her eyes. Light brown, or blond, if there was such a thing. A shade of brown so pale he'd never seen the likes before.

Her forehead scrunched and she chuckled. "Not really. This place isn't my thing," she said gently.

"You don't enjoy going out with friends?"

She sent him a look. One that said she knew what he was up to. "I do, just not to places like this."

"Where would you rather be?"

"Honestly? Probably at home watching *The Bachelor*."

Hunt let out a deep belly laugh. Could he have found a less compatible woman for himself? "My brother just took off to watch it with his wife."

She grinned. A genuine grin that transformed her pretty features into beautiful and did something to his chest, causing a pinching sensation. Not to mention the heat his body was suddenly radiating.

Okay, maybe they weren't so incompatible after all.

"Do you watch it too?" she asked.

"Not at all," Hunt said. "I'd rather be doing just about anything than watching reality television about romance."

She stared, seemingly forgetting her desire to not engage. "You should try it. It's about more than romance. Actually, romance might be secondary to the social experiment of turning the tables and making women the pursuers. It's highly entertaining."

"When you describe it like that, it does sound like something I'd enjoy." He gave her his award-winning smile.

And she shrank back.

Since when did his smile not melt panties from here to the border?

Since never.

Did he have something in his teeth? Nah, even that never stopped a woman from letting down her guard once he gave her the full force of the Cade grin, and he wasn't ashamed to use it.

She closed her eyes. "Let me stop you right there. I don't know what you have in mind, but I'm not interested."

Hunt pressed a palm above his heart. "Ouch. Not even a little?"

She laughed lightly. "Nope."

"Now that's harsh," he said, but he was smiling. She wasn't really his type either, but she was genuine, and he liked that. Most of the women Hunt spent time with were like Abby's friend. Beautiful and looking for a fun night. Honesty didn't factor into it.

"What if I'm the best man you'll ever meet?" Kind of a

lame line, but damn if he wasn't competitive. And Abby had thrown down the gauntlet by flat-out rejecting him.

She glanced up as though considering. "Well now, you could be. But here's the problem: I have baggage."

Hunt rolled his eyes. "Everyone has baggage."

"I have a dump truck's worth of baggage."

He leaned closer. "Now that is a lot. Care to share what this baggage entails? You never know, it might not bother me." Where the hell had that come from? Clearly, her rejection had thrown him out of his element. He didn't walk from women who needed more than he could give. He ran.

"Not particularly."

"Fair enough," he said. "So you'd never consider spending time with me because of said baggage, but you will watch *The Bachelor*, and, in fact, prefer it over socializing. Do I have that right?"

She tapped her index finger to her lips, and Hunt's gaze snagged on the pillowy softness. Her lips were distracting, and she wasn't even trying to seduce him. "That about sums up my life. But don't let it get you down. You're a good-looking guy." She scanned his frame. "Tall, with plenty of muscles beneath that button-up shirt, if I'm not mistaken. And you've got the chiseled, handsome look. And your eyes —wow. You've got beautiful eyes." She stared for a moment then blinked. "But I'm sure you've heard that before."

"Possibly." His eyes narrowed. "So if I'm such a fine specimen of manhood, why not take a chance?" Hunt wasn't sure he wanted a chance with this woman, but there was something about her... She was interesting and different from the women he usually spent time with.

"It's the baggage," she said matter-of-factly.

"Right," he said, "the baggage. Pretty heavy stuff, huh?"

She nodded. "The heaviest." And this time, her lighthearted attitude slipped. She bit the corner of her lip and looked away.

Hunt held back a frown, because he refused to frown when he was in his party element, which only made his jaw tighten with the false grin he held in place. If there was something Hunt couldn't handle, it was a sad woman. That was why he spent so much time trying to make them happy. Typically with his mouth and body.

And then something occurred to him. He was enjoying their conversation, but was she? "Is talking to me making you uncomfortable? Would you rather be alone?"

She looked up. "Honestly, I didn't come here to talk to men. I came because my friend wanted to check out the place. We work together, and I promised I'd go with her so she wouldn't be alone."

And that was his cue. He never turned down a challenge, but this woman truly wasn't interested. And he wasn't a complete caveman.

Hunt swigged the last of his drink and set it on the bar. He couldn't remove her baggage, but he could remove himself if it made her feel better. "I'm not one to bother a lady." He took her hand and gave it a light squeeze. "It was a pleasure meeting you, Abby. I'll leave you to your beer."

Hunt walked off in the direction of friends he'd noticed when he entered the place. His stride was long and confident, but his encounter with Abby left him off balance.

Most women he met at clubs and bars were looking for the kind of attention Hunt had to offer in droves. But not Abby. He would have liked to get to know her better. Of course, not in any serious way...

And at the same time, he couldn't imagine getting to know her in any other way.

CHAPTER TWO

When Hunt was seven, he wanted to become a pirate. Sure, he lived with his father and four brothers on a lake and not near an ocean, but *details*. He would become a pirate and save women on the high seas of Lake Tahoe. The antithesis of your typical pillaging pirate, but again, *details*. Hunt lost his mother at the age of one and a half and had no memory of her. What better purpose in life than to protect other mothers? And pretty girls—he'd decided that same summer he liked pretty girls.

When Hunt turned fourteen, he liked girls even more: the pretty ones, the sweet ones, the ones who wore glasses... and he worked hard to find out what they all wanted so he could give it to them. He carried their books between classes. He shoved letters into their lockers, rhapsodizing over their beauty, and it wasn't long before Hunt lost his virginity to one of those girls he so admired.

A few years later, Hunt's pirating skills were put to the test when he fell in love with a beautiful, vivacious woman.

There was only one problem. Lisa was a few years older

than Hunt, and the jerk trying to do his beloved harm was none other than Levi, Hunt's oldest brother.

Because Lisa was Levi's girlfriend at the time.

Hunt knew he was the worst man alive for falling in love with his brother's girl. Knew he was an even bigger ass for flirting with Lisa and giving her everything his older brother hadn't, as any good pirate would. But he couldn't help himself. And he couldn't have predicted the damage his love for Lisa would bring on his family.

Over a decade later, Levi still hadn't fully forgiven Hunt. But they'd made strides in getting over their estrangement. Levi had long since moved on, in particular with Emily, Lisa's younger sister. And how was that for irony?

Levi had fallen head over heels in love when Emily joined the management team at Club Tahoe. Going through that got Levi to acknowledge what a hard-ass he'd been to Hunt all these years, because no one was perfect. Not when Cupid played a part in matters.

Hunt had also moved on after that disaster of a first love. He was a Cade, after all, and Cade men didn't lack for female attention. But Hunt worked harder at achieving a woman's affection than his brothers, because he craved it.

Being with a woman—any woman—was essential to his well-being. As long as he didn't fall in love again. That had been the worst mistake he'd ever made, and nearly tore his family apart.

Hunt was fortunate that Abby had turned him down last night at the club. He wasn't sure what it was about her, but he suspected that had she allowed him to pursue her, he wouldn't have escaped unscathed.

Hunt's brothers were all he had. Oh, they fought like hell and argued constantly, but they had each other's backs. Always.

He lifted his arms over his head and stretched, glancing across the Club Tahoe beach he managed. It was close to six in the evening, and the sunbathers had gone inside to change for a night of fine dining and gambling at the Club Tahoe resort.

His favorite Club Kids patron walked toward him, kicking sand, his head bent down.

Hunt checked his phone. It was well past pick-up time. And unfortunately, it wasn't unusual for Noah to be the last one to leave the resort. "What's up, little man? Everything okay?"

Noah just turned five and had been coming to the club for several months now. Pretty soon the boy would be in school, but Hunt was hopeful that Noah's parents would continue sending him to the club's after-school and summer programs. Hunt had grown attached to the kid, and he wasn't eager to see the little guy go.

"My grandma isn't here," Noah said, his eyes glassy with unshed tears.

Hunt's chest pinched. If there was anything worse than seeing an unhappy woman, it was seeing a sad kid.

Hunt could easily relate to Noah, because he'd been that child left behind more times than he could count. He was the youngest of five brothers, with no mother, and a father who put work ahead of family. Hunt had learned at a young age to stick with his brothers or be left behind.

He squatted, putting himself at eye level with Noah. "Good, because I need your help cleaning up the beach and dock. What do you say?"

Noah looked suspicious, but then he glanced at the boat. A smile spread across his fair face, blond hair sticking up at odd angles. Noah loved the boats as much as Hunt, and Hunt used them to turn the end-of-day loneliness into a game for taking Noah's mind off things.

The little boy nodded, and they made their way to the dock right as Hunt's cell phone vibrated in his jeans pocket.

He glanced at the screen.

Chris: We're going out tonight. Just met the hottest chicks, and they're ready to party. Meet me at the entrance in fifteen.

Hunt pocketed his phone and put his hand on Noah's shoulder. "You know where the rags are? Grab one so you can help me wipe down the side of the boat." He really didn't need help polishing the boat, as he'd done it earlier, but it was one of Noah's favorite jobs. "Remember to keep your feet on the dock. No leaning over. I'm not up for fishing for Noahs tonight—water's cold."

Noah giggled and ran to the bucket of rags, set aside especially for this purpose. He picked up one and scrunched his nose. He tossed it then grabbed another and ran toward the boat.

Hunt shook his head. His "assistant" was becoming as particular as Hunt when it came to babying the boats—and it looked like Hunt needed to do a better job of getting the polishing cloths washed.

Hunt was in charge of beach and boating activities for Club Tahoe. Out of the four brothers who worked at the club, Hunt had the best job by far. Levi filled the role of CEO, and Hunt would rather be kicked in the teeth than deal with the stressful shit Levi put up with.

Hunt's middle brother Bran ran the restaurants. Again, fuck that job. Bran dealt with idiot servers calling in sick minutes before their shifts, and hangry (hungry and angry) customers. Then there was Wes, who ran the golf club-house and course. Wes and Hunt often collaborated on kid events now that the club had created a kids' golf program. Wes's job might be stressful from time to time, but he was a pro golfer. Somehow Hunt didn't think Wes suffered too much being in charge of the links.

Hunt had also taken on the role of helping plan kid events for the Club Kids program, because that shit was fun. Playing with kids, when he wasn't running boat tours for tourists and resort guests, kept the day moving along nicely.

Noah sank to his knees next to the old woody, the boat Hunt's father had purchased two decades ago as a throw-back to Lake Tahoe's early days. Club Tahoe owned other boats, but the woody was everyone's favorite.

"That's it," Hunt said. "Rub the side to a nice shine."

Hunt put away the bucket of rags and cleared a few things off the dock. He glanced across the beach. All the kids had gone home, and still no one had shown up for Noah.

Hunt motioned for one of the attendants near the Club Kids playroom.

Brin waved back, setting her clipboard aside. She walked quickly across the sand toward the dock.

"Good job, Noah," Hunt said. "Go ahead and toss the rag in the helm. We're all good here."

Hunt lifted the little boy onto the boat and Noah ran to the front. He threw the rag, and it landed on the steering wheel. Hunt had been teaching Noah boat vernacular, so he was damn proud the kid had gone in the right direction. They'd work out the specifics of orderliness later.

Hunt grabbed Noah and swung him back onto the dock. "Here's Brin."

The part-time college student/Club Kids worker

stepped onto the dock, a bright smile on her face as she peered at Noah.

Everyone was aware of Noah's flaky family, and they tried as a team to make things easier for him.

"Hey, Noah," Brin said. "Want to help me feed the animals before you head home? I could really use your help."

Noah looked up at Hunt.

"Go ahead, buddy. I've got an errand to run, but I'll be back."

Hunt watched Noah walk away with Brin, and he frowned. If he could smack Noah's parents upside the head and get them to appreciate their son, he would.

He made his way to the entrance of the resort to catch up with Chris, but his mind was still on Noah and the little boy's lack of reliable family.

"You got my text?" Chris said.

Hunt smiled at a family entering the club and stepped aside to let them pass. "I got it."

"You in?"

"Of course I'm in."

Chris eyed him. "Took you long enough; you never responded to my text."

"You're not my girlfriend. Simmer down." Noah came before any stupid shit Chris set up. So in some ways, yes, other things took priority over chasing women.

Hunt was closing in on thirty and helping his brothers run a multimillion-dollar resort, while Chris was a doorman Hunt went with to the clubs. Hunt might be a player, but he wasn't completely oblivious to what mattered in life.

Chris flicked a piece of lint off his Club Tahoe uniform. "Usually, you get back to me the moment I text about a hookup."

"Your point?" Hunt's gaze caught on a car that sputtered to a stop in front of the club.

"First you ditch me in the middle of picking up a hot chick at the bar last night, and now you're dragging your feet about going out. What was up with that, anyway? I had that hookup in the bag until you took off and left her friend stranded."

Hunt had played his role last night, but there were limits to what he was willing to do for a friend. Making a woman uncomfortable crossed the line. "I'm not forcing a dead end," Hunt said, his attention still on the clunker and the woman exiting it.

Her back was to him as she tucked a lock of light brown, wavy hair behind her ear and said something to the valet. She waved her hands, gesturing to the car and the entrance of the club.

"So that's what the problem was?" Chris said. "Some woman finally turned you down—"

And that was the moment Hunt tuned Chris out entirely. Because he caught a glimpse of the woman's face. She was flushed, but there was no mistaking it.

Hunt flagged the valet, and the man jogged over. "What's going on?"

"The woman's car broke down at the entrance. I told her she can't park there."

Hunt's blood pressure rose. "If her car broke down, she can't exactly move it. Go back and tell her you'll take care of it."

"I will? I-I mean," the valet stammered. "How?"

"Call the head of maintenance. See if he can get it started. If he can't, tell him to have it towed to Jeffery's Mechanic shop. The club will pay for the tow. This isn't some shoddy hotel. We take care of our customers."

The valet ran back to the woman and appeared to apologize.

Her arms were wrapped around her waist, and she nodded. And then she looked in Hunt's direction, and, for some stupid reason, he didn't look away.

Abby met Hunt's gaze, and her mouth parted in surprise.

She was wearing scrubs—which explained the clogs from last night.

"Hunt?" Chris snapped his fingers in Hunt's face. "You still there?"

Hunt glared at Chris. "Do that again and you'll lose a digit."

Chris held up his hands. "Relax, man." He glanced in the direction Hunt had been staring. "Who's that woman? She looks familiar."

"No one," Hunt said, but in his periphery, he watched Abby enter the club, rushing through the door the valet held for her.

"Ah," Chris said, nodding and looking between Abby and her car. "I get it. You're one of those chivalrous bastards. That's how you get all the women."

Hunt turned his attention to his pseudo-friend who was becoming less of a friend every day. "If women like me, it's because I give them what they want. And I'm nice to them. You should try it sometime."

Chris laughed. "Whatever. See you at ten in the Sky Lounge."

Hunt entered the lobby, but Abby was nowhere to be found.

When he returned to Club Kids, Noah was gone too.

For a split second, Hunt wondered if Abby had picked up his favorite club kid, but she hadn't mentioned having a child. Only baggage. And Hunt didn't consider kids baggage. If Noah was Abby's kid... Well, it was best he never got to know her, because that was something even his loose morals couldn't abide. He'd never spend time with a woman who left her child behind.

As far as Hunt knew, Noah got picked up by his grandparents. Abby had to be here for some other reason. And given he couldn't find her, it looked like Hunt would never know what it was.

CHAPTER THREE

Abby was putting in another twelve-hour day, dog-tired after covering her own shift plus part of another LVN's who'd called in sick.

She'd been in classes to become a registered nurse when her life had taken a sharp turn. Now she was left with long shifts as a licensed vocational nurse and so much responsibility that her dream of completing her nursing degree had faded years ago. She wondered on days like today, when everything seemed to be going wrong, if she'd ever manage to come up for air.

"Abby," Noah's paternal grandmother, Vivian, said over the phone. "We won't be able to pick up your son today."

Abby nearly choked on the caffeinated soda she'd been chugging during her short break. "But I'm pulling a long shift."

"Are you telling me you can't handle being a mother? This is *your* job. But I've said it before and I'll say it again: Trevor's father and I would be more than happy to shoulder the responsibility of Noah's upbringing if you were to pursue your career."

In other words, if Abby wanted to give up custody of her son.

No way. Not ever.

After Trevor's sudden death when Noah was a baby, nothing else mattered except caring for her young child. "I have things under control."

But she didn't. Not really.

Abby got off the phone and clenched her teeth. Vivian had been kind and sweet when her boyfriend Trevor was alive. Now his mother was an entirely different person. Loss could hit people like that sometimes, and it seemed that was what had happened to Vivian.

Everything, including Trevor's checking account, froze the day he died. The deed for his home was in his parents' names. So even though Abby lived with Trevor, she was forced to move, unable to pay his parents the rent they demanded. That was around the time Abby realized just how far Vivian was willing to go to hold on to the last shred of her son.

Abby ended up quitting nursing school, getting a full-time job, and moving into a tiny cabin she and Noah lived in to this day. She was barely able to make ends meet, but as long as she worked double shifts from time to time, she managed.

Abby returned calls to patients who'd reached out to their doctors as quickly as she could, and left work early. Again. But there was no way around it. There was no room for error when it came to raising Noah. Vivian was too eager in the wings, ready to pounce the moment Abby screwed up.

She made her way to her crappy car and headed to Noah's daycare. God, she hated being late for her son. There was never enough time to work, take care of household chores, and spend quality time with Noah. She worried he didn't know how much she loved him. Worried he didn't know that he was her entire world.

Abby neared Club Tahoe's entrance, idling for a moment as a family exited in front of her, then pulled forward. But because this day had sucked hard and didn't seem to be getting any better, her car took that moment to keel over and die in front of the fancy resort.

Crap.

Abby stepped out of her car and tried to explain to the valet her vehicle's spotty history and how it sometimes died. That given five or ten minutes, it would fire up again. The valet wasn't having any of it.

Until he glanced at something—or *someone*—over her shoulder. "One moment, please." The valet took off and Abby looked at the time. She wrapped her arms around her waist, frustrated with her unreliable car and worried about Noah.

When the valet returned a moment later, his entire expression had softened. "I'll have your car taken care of, ma'am. Go ahead inside."

"You will? I mean—you're sure?"

"Yes, ma'am." He gestured for her to go inside the entrance.

Abby took the favor for what it was, a godsend, and hurried toward the front doors of Club Tahoe. But not before she scanned the area where the valet had run off.

And saw Hunt, the handsome man from last night.

What in the world?

Hunt had been his friend's "second" so the other guy could talk to Abby's beautiful workmate. But what had begun as an obligation to talk to Hunt while her coworker spoke to his friend turned into something more natural and less forced as they chatted. She'd nearly lost herself in the conversation, until she realized spending time with men like Hunt would never be an option. Not while her son was young and needed her.

She'd caught a look of disappointment on his face when she explained she really wasn't interested, and though she regretted turning him away, it had been the right thing to do. She was sure of it.

Nearly sure. Mostly sure.

It had been a long time since a man had shown any interest in Abby. She was shocked she'd had the strength to not cave to his handsome face and sexy smile. Really, it had been a feat of immense strength when she thought back. She may have been celibate since Trevor died, but it wasn't for lack of missing someone in her life. Her son and work simply filled up all her free time.

She looked away, her face hot with embarrassment. Of course her car would die in front of *this* man.

It was a strange coincidence to run into Hunt the day after she met him, but she didn't have time to figure it out. If he'd played a part in helping her with her car just now, she owed him. And she'd worry about that later.

CHAPTER FOUR

Hunt woke with the mother of all hangovers. He'd been on a mission last night to fog his brain with alcohol, and damn if he hadn't succeeded.

Pain shot through his head, and he winced as he turned and glanced at the warm body next to him.

He had left the lounge Chris dragged him to last night with a woman named Jade, who was now lying beside him. They'd gone to her place, where he'd given her an orgasm and then proceeded to pass out. He hadn't even needed a condom. Hadn't been in the mood for sex. If he thought about it, he'd taken Jade home last night—or rather to her home, given he never brought anyone to his place—in order to get the hell out of the lounge without having to explain to Chris why he was leaving early. Because it wasn't normal for Hunt to leave early from a night out and go home alone.

Something was off. But he couldn't figure out what it was.

He shook his head and instantly regretted it. Pinching his brow until the pain receded, he reached over the side of the bed for his clothes. It was five in the morning and still dark. Without a word, he slipped from the bed and left the room.

Jade lived in an apartment near Stateline. No roommates, thank God. Hunt pulled on his clothes in the living room and left her a note on the kitchen counter next to a box of strawberry Pop-Tarts.

> *Jade,*
> *Thank you for last night.*

No signature. And he never left his phone number. Didn't want calls from women he had no intention of seeing again.

Maybe she'd forget his name. Women didn't seem to mind a one-night stand with him. He showed them a good time, treated them with respect, but he never led women to believe there'd be anything more.

A few times he'd run into past flings, and they had always been happy to see him. And eager for round two. Which he was careful to avoid. Spending more than one night with someone led to expectations, and he never wanted to give a woman the wrong impression.

Jade had been exactly the type of woman Hunt favored. Someone looking for a good time, no strings attached. And in a few hours, he'd forget all about her.

Meanwhile, he couldn't get Abby and her car out of his head, and it was bugging the crap out of him. He hadn't even kissed her the night they'd met at the club, let alone slept with her. So why did she keep popping into his mind?

———

LATER THAT MORNING, Hunt learned that the head of maintenance at Club Tahoe had sent Abby's beater car to Jeffery's Mechanic shop because he'd been unable to get the car started.

"Alternator," the maintenance guy said.

"Those are expensive," Hunt murmured to himself.

The head of maintenance grunted.

For a fraction of a second, Hunt wondered if he should pay for the car to be fixed. He could afford it, but why the hell was he thinking of doing it? He was courteous toward women—he paid for meals and any entertainment when they were out—but this was beyond courteous. He didn't know Abby. Literally didn't know her last name.

Of course he shouldn't pay for her car.

Hunt pushed thoughts of Abby aside and prepared the pontoon for a lake cruise scheduled that afternoon. When he returned a few hours later, he cleaned up the boat and made his way to Club Kids for his late afternoon round of play-with-whatever-kids-were-hanging-until-their-parents-got-off-work.

It was his favorite time of the day, but he'd never tell his brothers how much he loved working with the kids. They'd say it was because he was a giant child at heart. Which wasn't entirely off base. But to share the other reasons he enjoyed spending time with the kids would reveal a part of him that was personal. And honestly, his brothers would never believe him anyway. They had one image of who he was, and nothing would change that. Hunt knew, because he'd tried.

It had been a while since he had scheduled a kids versus Club Kids attendants tug-of-war. Time for a new round, winner got ice cream.

Kaylee, Wes's wife, had returned from an extended

maternity leave to continue running the Club Kids program, now that their daughter Harlow was old enough to come along too. She stood off to the side, talking to one of the helpers, and Hunt swooped in and picked up Harlow from the baby area where one of the attendants was playing with her.

He nuzzled kisses on Harlow's neck rolls—who was feeding this child, anyway?—and Harlow laughed and smacked his head with her chubby baby hands.

His niece liked to bat her uncles around. And they all allowed it because she was the only girl in two generations of Cades. As far as Hunt was concerned, she was a princess, and he and his brothers would treat her as such.

"Huuunnt," he said, looking into Harlow's eyes, trying to imprint his name in her mind.

He and his brothers had a running bet over whose name Harlow would say first. She was already saying "momma" and "dada," but the rest was up for grabs. Hunt, Bran, Levi, and Adam made it a point to repeat their names to Harlow every chance they got. The winner got a round of beers.

His family had enough money to live in luxury for more than a lifetime, but they were Cades. The kitty could be a penny, and he and his brothers would fight to the death to claim it. No challenge was too small.

Hunt repeated his name again, despite Harlow batting him across the head every time he did it, laughing.

"That's cheating."

Hunt glanced up to see Kaylee standing there with her hands on her hips.

He focused back on Harlow. "It's not cheating. I need to make sure she practices."

Kaylee smiled at Harlow—and stole her from Hunt's arms.

Dammit. It was hard as hell to get in Harlow time when his siblings, or her mother, were around. Which was always.

Kaylee propped Harlow on her hip. "Stop harassing my baby," she said, and gave him a look.

Every last one of his brothers had settled down, the idiots. And, of course, they had to choose strong women who gave Hunt a hard time, just like his brothers. Which only meant Hunt had to sneak in his Harlow training when Kaylee wasn't around.

"Sure, sure. Whatever you say, Kaylee." He sent her his most charming smile. Only it hadn't worked with Abby. She'd been a bizarre exception he hoped wouldn't become the norm.

Kaylee glared. "That dimpled grin won't work on me. Your brother has hardened me to Cade charm."

Hunt sighed. "What has he done now?"

Kaylee kissed her daughter's forehead. "Wes hasn't done anything. Yet. But I've learned to stay on my toes around that man."

"Wes would do anything for you."

Kaylee blew a lock of dark hair out of her eye and shifted her daughter to the other hip. "Damn straight, after what he put me through before we got married."

No argument there. Wes had ruined his relationship with Kaylee when they'd dated in college, and he nearly did it again years later the second time around. Fortunately for Wes, he'd gotten his shit together and made Kaylee his priority. And Harlow. Hunt never thought he'd see the day, but his brother doted on his little girl and was an excellent father.

Hunt reached out to tickle Harlow's belly and mouthed his name, hoping Kaylee was too busy motioning for one of the Club Kids attendants to notice.

Quick as a rattlesnake, Kaylee slapped his hand away. "Did you come here to try my patience, or was there a purpose to your visit?"

Damn, she was quick. "I came to check on the kids and see if you needed help. I've got the last couple of hours free."

Kaylee's shoulders sank. "That's more like it. Yes, I need help. This place has doubled in size since I went on maternity leave. We're bursting at the seams. My first priority is to hire more attendants. In the meantime, do you mind helping Brin watch the kids? And keep an eye on the older ones. Some of them can get rough."

Hunt rolled his eyes. "Wes ever tell you about our childhood? We defined rough play."

Kaylee's lips pursed. "Good point. Okay, have at it. Brin is lining the children up by the door while I put together a craft project for the little ones."

He notched his head at Harlow. "I can take her with me if you need your arms free."

"No! Now get out of here before you brainwash my daughter."

Hunt chuckled and followed the kids out the door, making sure to grab the tug-of-war rope.

An hour later, ice cream won by the kids after the horde of them pummeled Hunt and Brin in tug-of-war, Hunt was hunched in the sand, creating a sandcastle masterpiece.

"Noah," Hunt said. "Our castle needs a flag. Gotta let everyone know who owns it."

Noah scrunched his face. "How do I make a flag? We don't have paper and crayons out here."

"We have something better," Hunt said. "Grab one of the buffing rags I left on the dock this afternoon. Make sure to get one that has the Club Tahoe emblem. Also, look for a nice, straight stick on your way."

Noah smiled and jumped up with the energy only a five-year-old had.

Hunt grinned and continued working on the sandcastle, helping out the other kids and praising their work. He scanned the beach to make sure all the children were accounted for, and caught sight of his brother Bran making his way over from Prime, the club's award-winning steak and seafood restaurant.

Hunt climbed to his feet and dusted sand off his pants. "How's it going?" Hunt said, and looked around. Noah was taking a while, but he caught sight of the boy at the end of the dock near the bucket of rags, sifting through each one, probably looking for the perfect flag.

Hunt chuckled. His assistant was a perfectionist.

"You got time to talk or are you too distracted by the new lifeguard?" Bran glanced at the lifeguard in question.

Hunt hadn't been the least bit focused on Gabrielle, but his brothers assumed the worst of him. Always.

The new lifeguard was doing a great job. She was super attentive and on top of making sure the kids behaved safely. As soon as Hunt realized she had a good handle on things, he'd forgotten all about her. But Hunt's brothers thought him female-crazed. And he couldn't argue their point. When he wasn't working, he sought all the female attention he could get. He also worried about the club as much as they did, and would never date someone he hired. Not that any of them believed it. "Gabrielle is on the college swim team. I hired her for her skills."

Bran snorted. "Sure you did. Has nothing to do with the fact she's a perfect ten?"

"Where's Ireland?" Hunt said. "I thought she was the

only woman you looked at?" Bran had gone from a monk, living without sex for years, to a devoted boyfriend. Talk of Ireland was a sure way to distract him.

"My beautiful girlfriend is on her way. We have plans—"

Hunt tuned out his brother, his attention suddenly focused on a flash of orange near the dock.

And then Hunt was running into the lake, where he scooped Noah up from the cold water.

"You okay, buddy?" he said as he cradled Noah against his shoulder, holding him close.

Noah buried his face in Hunt's neck and silently cried.

"It's okay. I've got you."

Brin ran over with a towel, along with Gabrielle. "What happened?" Brin said.

Hunt jerked his thumb over his shoulder. "New kid in the orange T-shirt shoved Noah off the dock."

"I saw it happen," Gabrielle said, "but I was too far away to stop it."

"James." Brin's eyebrows knitted, and she covered Noah with the towel. "I'll talk to him," she said, and walked in the boy's direction.

"Noah okay?" Gabrielle asked. She touched Noah's back, and he burrowed deeper into Hunt's shoulder.

Hunt shifted his head to try to get a look at Noah, who was clinging to him like a barnacle. "I think so. I'm just gonna take him for a walk." He wrapped the towel around Noah tighter. "Keep an eye on the others, will you?"

"Of course," Gabrielle said. She turned and blew her whistle loud enough to burst eardrums, and corralled the kids.

Bran was wrong about Hunt's intentions. Gabrielle *was* attractive. Young, with an athletic figure. But Hunt hadn't hired her for her looks. That girl had kicked ass on the brutal swimming challenge he'd required of all applicants for the lifeguard position. She'd passed with flying colors. And she'd been compassionate with the kids. *That* was why he'd hired her.

Gabrielle made the kids pick up sand toys and return to the Club Kids room.

Bran and Ireland walked up to Hunt and Noah. "Everything okay?" Ireland asked, her expression concerned.

Hunt nodded and waved his hand in an "I'll catch you later" motion. Noah was a bubbly guy. It wasn't like him to cry, and Hunt wanted to make sure he was okay without an audience, even if it was just Bran and Ireland.

He walked down the beach a ways, rubbing Noah's back. "How're you doing, little man?"

"He shoved me," Noah shakily murmured.

"I saw it."

"He said I was in his way."

Hunt sighed. "What he did isn't okay. Ever. Especially near water. Brin's talking to him now, and I'll make sure we talk to all the kids. We don't shove or take chances near the water."

Hunt felt Noah relax a fraction.

"The big kids always pick on me." Noah leaned back and looked at Hunt with the saddest eyes Hunt had ever seen.

"Sometimes kids aren't nice to each other," Hunt said. "But that doesn't mean you should get back at them. Continue to treat others how you want to be treated. But walk away if they're being aggressive." Jesus, he sounded like Esther, his dad's former receptionist, and the only mother figure he and his brothers ever had.

Esther, and a couple of other faithful Club Tahoe

employees, were probably the only reason Hunt and his brothers turned out to be halfway-decent human beings.

After a fifteen-minute walk, where Hunt distracted Noah with talk of plans for the boats, Hunt returned to Club Kids with a now-smiling Noah walking beside him.

Most of the kids had been picked up, but Noah's ride was nowhere in sight. As usual.

Hunt stretched his neck, his body tensing. Brin would have called Noah's emergency contact to inform them of what happened. You'd think that on a day like today the guardian in charge could have shown up on time for once.

Hunt was grateful he'd been there for Noah, but his heart pounded just from thinking about how much worse things could have been. Noah could have fallen headfirst into knee-deep water. With a fall like that, the boy could have broken his neck.

Kids had accidents. Thankfully, they bounced back well. But Hunt couldn't stop his mind from racing with every possible worst-case scenario.

Was this what it was like to be a parent? A real parent, not the kind his father had been. Absent, frustrated, uncaring. But someone who actually wanted to be there for his kid? Because this sucked.

Hunt would die an early death due to worry if he ever had a kid of his own. He'd lost a couple of years off his life in the split second it took him to reach Noah, and Noah wasn't even his child.

He squeezed Noah's hand, reassuring himself that the boy was okay. All this worry had to be the *Harlow Effect.* His baby niece came into his life, and he'd experienced a love he never had before. He'd protect Harlow with his life, and it seemed that protective instinct was rubbing off in other areas as well.

Hunt considered himself more sensitive to kids, having lost his mother at such a young age. It was almost as if she'd never existed. But she had. She'd held off chemotherapy so that Hunt, growing inside her, could survive. His mother's sacrifice was something Hunt had never been able to come to terms with. Because it wasn't only Hunt who'd lost a mother due to her decision to hold off chemo; his brothers lost one too. And Hunt never stopped feeling the guilt for that decision.

"Where's my mom?" Noah said.

Noah was sitting beside Hunt on one of the picnic benches near Club Kids. "I thought you lived with your grandparents?" Hunt said.

"Noooo," Noah said, shaking his head. "I live with my mom, silly."

"I'm silly? Who's the one who dumped sand down Brin's jacket?"

Noah giggled. "You're sillyyy!" he chanted.

Clearly the boy was feeling better. "So your mom—"

"There she is!" Noah jumped up from the picnic table and ran toward the back of the lobby that exited near the pool.

And that was when Hunt's heart dropped. Or raced... sputtered—whatever.

Because Noah's mom was Abby.

CHAPTER FIVE

Abby swept Noah into her arms and peppered his face with kisses, breathing in his sweaty boy scent after a day at Club Kids. The crap she put up with at work, the threats from Noah's grandparents...it all melted away the moment she held her son.

He was getting so big. Pretty soon she wouldn't be able to get away with picking him up or kissing the heck out of him. For now, she stole all the kisses she could.

Abby held Noah as he jabbered on about his day, taking in his ruffled hair and...soaked clothes? "Why are you wet?" The moisture was seeping through her scrubs, making her wet as well.

Noah's smile sank and his chin began to wobble. "A boy pushed me off the dock."

"*He what?*" Abby looked toward the Club Kids playroom—and caught sight of a familiar face. One she hadn't expected to ever see again after the night they met, and yet she kept running into him.

Hunt sat at a bench watching them. It had been odd

seeing him yesterday when her car had broken down, but today as well?

She headed to the Club Kids playroom and stopped in front of Hunt. "What's going on?"

Was he stalking her? He hadn't seemed stalkerish the other night. In fact, he'd left her alone when she told him she wasn't interested. She'd met plenty of men who would have pursued her regardless, unable to resist a challenge.

Abby was willing to bet Hunt had helped her with her car yesterday too. One minute the valet at Club Tahoe was harassing her about moving the thing, and the next minute he was helping her get it towed. After he'd spoken to Hunt.

Hunt continued to watch her and Noah, and he didn't look happy. What was that about?

"I work here," he said. What are *you* doing here?"

"Picking up my son from his daycare. But it seems he had a rough day." Understatement, but she didn't want to get upset in front of Noah. And if Hunt really worked here, he'd receive an earful from her soon enough.

She'd assumed that by sending Noah to Club Tahoe— one of the most respected establishments in the area, with a daycare center parents raved about—her child would be safe while she worked to keep them sheltered, with food on the table. Apparently not.

She took a deep breath and shifted gears. No need to jump to conclusions. "Was Noah getting pushed today an accident?"

Hunt grabbed the back of his neck without meeting her eyes. "Not exactly," he said, at the same time Noah shook his head.

Abby saw red. Kids sometimes played rough. That didn't mean they acted in malice. But apparently, this kid had intentionally hurt her child.

This was *her son*, and she paid a pretty penny—one she couldn't afford—for him to attend Club Kids. She expected a hell of a lot better than her child being shoved off a dock. Her son could have hit his head and drowned.

She sent a harsh look at Hunt then glanced at her son. "What happened?"

Noah's eyes darted away. "Sometimes the bigger kids pick on the little ones, and I'm the smallest. Except for the babies. But they don't play with us."

That was it. She didn't care how good of a reputation Club Tahoe had; it wasn't the place for her child. "Come on. Let's grab your things. We're leaving."

———

AFTER ANNOUNCING THEY WERE LEAVING, Abby looked at Hunt and shot darts from her eyes. Or would have, if darts could shoot from eyes.

Hunt couldn't blame her for being upset about the kid pushing Noah. *Hunt* was upset. But why would this woman show up late if she cared so much about her kid? No matter how heartwarming the greeting, anyone who didn't pick up their child on time after a traumatizing event was suspect, in Hunt's book.

Brin had talked to all the kids that afternoon and gave them the whole "gentle bodies" speech, as Kaylee called it when she went into child psychologist mode. Meaning, keep your hands to yourself and don't hurt others. But Hunt was upset it had happened at all. He never wanted to see Noah hurt, or any kid for that matter. Which was ironic.

Hunt and his brothers grew up picking on each other and getting into daily physical fights. It was how he'd been raised. Basically, like animals in polo shirts and khakis without a mother or attentive father to teach them right from wrong. They'd eventually grown out of the physical fighting—*for the most part*—but Hunt didn't want that for Noah. Noah was a gentle soul, and kids picking on him could crush the little guy.

Before the boy ran off, he smiled at Hunt. "That's my mom," he said proudly, and darted toward Club Kids.

Clearly, Noah loved his mom. And regardless of whether or not she showed up on time—which still irked Hunt—she appeared to love her boy too.

Hunt sent her the same smile that *hadn't* worked on her the other night, eager to smooth things over.

Except Abby's scowl deepened.

What the hell? His smile hadn't worked on this woman. Twice now. That was a record, and not one he wished to triplicate.

"How could you allow some bully to push Noah into the water?" she said. "What kind of place are you running?"

Hunt glanced around. "A pretty nice one, considering the reviews." His comment hadn't helped. Her plush lips pursed. Still kissable, though. "Rest assured," he said, "we've talked to the child who pushed Noah. Nothing's more important than water safety around here."

"Hunt took me on a walk after it happened," Noah said, darting in front of Hunt and wrapping his arms around his mother's waist, apparently catching the tail end of their conversation.

"I didn't know you had a son," Hunt said, finally pointing out the elephant in the room. "You didn't mention it the other night."

"You saw me here yesterday. I'm sure you didn't forget my car breaking down."

He remembered. He just hadn't believed she, of all

women, could be his favorite kid's mother. "Did Jeffery's fix the car?"

Her shoulders sank in a deep sigh. "They did. Thank you for helping me. But this?" She waved her hands at the lake and Noah. "It's not okay. I'm sorry, but this won't work out anymore for Noah."

"*Mom*," Noah said, staring at his mother in horror.

She glanced at her son as though conflicted, resting her hand on his shoulder. "I'm sorry, honey. I know you like it here, but I need you to be safe." She turned to Hunt. "I paid the exorbitant fees for Club Kids because I thought it was the best for Noah. But if he's getting bullied—"

"It *is* the best," Noah argued. "I learn lots of stuff. Hunt teaches me about boats, and I get to help him work on them."

Hunt cleared his throat. "Noah helps me buff the sides of the boats. Always within my view. And he's a big help." Hunt made sure to send an approving nod to Noah.

"That's...nice," she said. "I'm sure it's been fun for him. But I can't take a chance on anything else happening to my son."

"I agree," Hunt said.

"I—You do?" Abby looked flustered, as though she hadn't expected those words.

"I don't want anything to happen to Noah or any of the children, which is why we're hiring more attendants to keep an eye on each child." Okay, so that had been Kaylee's idea, but she'd been right. Club Kids had boomed and they needed more help. "I can assure you that your son is in the best hands while here."

For some reason, the idea of Noah leaving Club Kids brought a sour taste to Hunt's mouth. He didn't want to see the boy go. He just needed to convince Noah's mother that he'd be safe.

"And I believe you're sincere," she said, "but the program is expensive. I can find the same ratio of workers to children somewhere else. Someplace where my son won't be in danger of drowning."

First Abby turned him down when he hit on her the other night at the bar. Then his powerhouse smile hadn't worked today when he tried to reassure her, and his smile was foolproof. He ignored the blip with Kaylee earlier because she married Wes, and clearly his brother had taught Kaylee to be skeptical. Now, Abby was rejecting Hunt's smooth-talking assurances? What the hell?

Hunt was the smooth brother. Okay, fine, that was his opinion. But obviously he had a way with ladies even his brothers couldn't deny. Only today was proving to be particularly harsh. Or maybe it was Abby. She'd been the one constant these last few days.

There was nothing higher on Hunt's priority list than making a woman feel safe. Had the world turned upside down? Was Mercury in retrograde? What was happening this week?

Women didn't reject him. Not once he put his mind on winning them over.

Wait, *had* he planned to win Abby over? He hadn't when they met at the club. But now that he knew she was Noah's mother, he wanted...something. Maybe it was simply more time to convince her that Noah was safe at Club Kids. Noah was a part of the gang. There had to be a way to make things right.

Hunt and his brothers had been taught water safety early on. Their father had hired a damned ex-Navy SEAL to teach them boating, and the man had hammered safety into their thick skulls. He could keep the kids safe. Abby just needed to give him a chance.

Noah pressed his face into his mother's stomach and appeared to be crying.

"Abby," Hunt said. He wasn't trying to woo her this time. He wanted to make things right. So he spoke from the heart, something he wasn't used to. "I understand your concern, but kids aren't perfect. They get into fights and they make mistakes. It's our job at the club to not only show them a good time and introduce them to new experiences, but also to socialize them and be a guiding hand." Jesus, he really needed to stop hanging around Kaylee. He sounded like a kindergarten teacher. "Why don't I walk you to the Club Kids playroom? We can talk about it some more there."

She paused, then shook her head.

"I'm sorry, I just can't risk it. Today is Noah's last day."

CHAPTER SIX

No one understood the pressure Abby was under with Trevor's parents. It would take hours to explain what had happened since her boyfriend died, so she didn't bother trying.

Hunt waved over a woman in a Club Kids polo shirt. "Brin, can you take Noah to the diner for a root beer float?"

"Mom?" Noah said hopefully.

Hunt knew her son. Noah was crazy for root beer floats. He'd be bouncing off the walls afterward, but he'd had a rough day and she couldn't deny him. She stroked the top of his head. "Sure, honey."

This was clearly Hunt's way of getting her alone. She didn't mind, because she had a few choice words to get off her chest as well. Namely, why someone hadn't stopped the child today from picking on her son. She didn't believe for one moment that it was an isolated incident, as Hunt had suggested.

As soon as Noah was out of earshot, Abby spoke first, before Hunt had a chance to convince her to keep Noah in the program. "Putting aside the fact that you have a bullying situation here, I can't afford the Club Kids cost any longer." She wrapped her arms around her waist. "It's too expensive, and now Noah has been physically harmed. He said the kids pick on him. How could you let this happen?"

Hunt's jaw clenched. "As I said, sometimes kids get rough, but we don't condone that behavior. The incident today was addressed with the child right after it occurred. In the future, we'll take every measure necessary to make sure situations like this don't happen again. I can't promise that children will always be nice to one another, but I can promise to address it whenever it occurs."

She shook her head. "It doesn't matter. Noah won't be here."

More tightening of the jaw. "Because of the cost?" he asked.

Admitting her financial constraints was humiliating. "Yes, in part. I also can't risk anyone so much as harming a hair on Noah's head while under my care."

Hunt's eyes narrowed. "You're going to have a tough time with that one. Noah is a kind kid, but even he's been known to throw sand at other children. As for the cost of monthly enrollment, we've just established a scaled payment plan. Whatever your income, we can accommodate it."

"I—You can?" This was the first she'd heard of a scaled payment plan at Club Tahoe. Was he feeling sorry for her? Making accommodations because she clearly couldn't handle things?

That was all she needed, for her incompetence to be broadcast to everyone. If the community agreed with Vivian —that Abby wasn't fit to parent her son—she'd have no hope.

Abby squeezed her eyes shut, the familiar burn of tears

forming behind her eyelids. She wouldn't cry. Not in front of Hunt, the handsome man who, had she been carefree and younger, she would have given in to at the club. Just as she'd given in to sweet, charming Trevor.

She had her son. She'd never regret the short time she'd spent with Trevor, or the consequences she paid for daily in the form of his parents.

She looked up and blinked, clearing her eyes. "I appreciate what you're doing, but I'm a single mother, and I'm currently working double shifts to support us. I can't sustain that much longer." Noah needed her. Somehow, she had to work less and still pay the bills. "Even with a reduced fee, I couldn't swing it." It was even more humiliating to admit she couldn't afford the reduced cost.

Without even pausing, Hunt said, "If you can't afford it, we'll accommodate."

Her eyes widened in disbelief. "No one gives away free daycare."

"Noah is a part of the Club Kids crew. If he and his family need our support, we're here for him."

Here for her son, or...? No, of course this wasn't about her. Why would Hunt be interested in her—a single mom with perpetual dark circles under eyes?

Super hot. She mentally laughed at where her thoughts had gone. Stress and raising her child alone had given her telltale signs of exhaustion no amount of napping fixed. She'd need an entire month of sleep to catch up.

So she was his charity case. Perfect. But there were other things to consider. "Thank you. It's very kind, but I can't."

What if news got back to Noah's grandparents that she couldn't afford daycare? Could they somehow use that against her? Vivian had threatened to take Noah from her so many times, and in so many ways, that anything seemed possible.

Hunt huffed out a breath. "I've eliminated the cost issue. And we've discussed the fact that our team is hiring more hands to make sure the kids are safe as the program grows. What else could there be?"

So much more.

She dropped her hands to her sides, and a sneaky tear fell. Great, just great. Now she looked financially desperate *and* weak. She swiped her cheek quickly and plastered on a smile.

Hunt gently gripped her elbow. She allowed him to lead her to a quiet corner in the lobby. "What is going on, Abby?"

The way he spoke to her, as if he knew her, it was... disarming. She wanted to unload all on him, but she couldn't. If he didn't seem so determined to keep Noah in the program, and if Noah didn't really love the guy, she wouldn't have shared what she had.

"Noah is a good kid. I'd like to help," Hunt said.

She sent him a side-glance. "You've done more than you needed to. The car. Offering to remove the cost of the program. But I can't accept any more help. It might hurt me and Noah in the long run." At his confused expression, she added, "It's a long story."

He leaned forward in the chair across from her, resting his elbows on his knees. "I've got time."

She should feel self-conscious. He'd seen that stupid tear streak down her face, for heaven's sake, but Hunt wasn't the charming playboy he'd been at the bar the other night. With those beautiful turquoise eyes looking at her so intently, he appeared genuinely concerned.

Those eyes were a menace.

Even without the eyes, Hunt was extremely persuasive. It was his words, his confident manner, and the way her body leaned toward him when he was near, as though it recognized something it liked. It was a good thing Abby had put a lockdown on her hormones and barely noticed the opposite sex.

Noah's father had been tall and not as muscular as Hunt, but he'd been handsome and charming too. And gentle, like her son.

Hunt didn't look gentle. He was muscular, with a strong jawline and those insane blue eyes. But whatever spark she felt around him, it was eviscerated as soon as she visualized middle-of-the-night wake-up calls from Noah when he'd had a bad dream or vomited on her clothes while sick. No man in his prime would want anything to do with Abby. Not when he could just as easily find a fun, attractive woman without her problems.

"My boyfriend's mother wants to take my son away from me," she said. There, that should frighten him off. He thought she only had money troubles? He didn't know the half of it.

"What does your boyfriend have to say about that?"

"He's dead."

Hunt blinked and looked away. "I'm sorry. That must be hard on you and Noah."

"It is. Though Noah doesn't remember his father. He died when Noah was a year old. A rock-climbing accident." It had been life-shattering at the time. She hadn't known how to survive without Trevor. Four years later, she knew how she'd survive: by scraping and clawing her way through life and praying she'd keep it all together.

She missed Trevor, but she'd be lying if she said she didn't feel a tinge of resentment that he'd dragged things out and not married her as soon as she told him she was pregnant. "We'll get married after the baby is born," Trevor had said when she was four months along. "That way you won't have to worry about wedding planning while you're pregnant."

Months passed and Trevor never brought it up again. When Abby mentioned setting a date for the wedding six months after Noah's birth, Trevor had told her he had to figure out the financials with his parents. He wanted her to sign a prenup, and she'd been fine with it. But Trevor never got around to setting anything up. He died soon after that conversation, leaving her and their son destitute.

Trevor's passing was an accident. But he'd always liked a good adrenaline rush, and rock climbing without a harness or safety lines had been the ultimate rush. Now he was gone, and his son had paid the price. The last thing Trevor's parents would do was help Abby out. They wanted her to crash and burn so they could gain custody of their only son's child.

Hunt rubbed his eyes. "I'm sorry," he said again.

"We're okay." Abby was so used to chanting it mentally that the words came out automatically.

Hunt looked up. "I wouldn't want that for any child—to lose a parent so young."

She nodded, holding back more emotion from leaking out. She'd been stressed this week. That had to explain the tear that had escaped without her permission.

Noah burst into the lobby, followed by Brin, a big smile on his face. "Mom!" He ran over and flung himself across her lap, his legs going up dramatically in a crash landing.

Abby held on to her son, ducking from long limbs precariously close to her head. "How was the root beer float?"

"Best ever!" he said. He twisted his head toward Hunt. "Did you convince my mom to let me stay?"

"Noah," she said warningly.

"I'm working on it," Hunt said, and winked at him.

Working on it? She'd made it clear this would never work. Hunt was a stubborn man. If he wasn't so good with her son, she might be annoyed.

She glanced at the time. It was late and she still needed to make dinner. "We'd better get going." She stood and grabbed Noah's backpack.

Brin hugged Noah goodbye, and he squeezed her in return.

He is loved here. If things weren't so bad, she'd give Club Tahoe another chance.

Hunt rose from the chair. "Will you consider my offer? We'd love to continue having Noah in the program. Give me a day or two, and I'll send you paperwork so that the financial aspect is off the table. You can make your decision from there."

She sent him a half-smile, but there was nothing to think about.

Abby walked out the door with Noah at her side.

CHAPTER SEVEN

S he was crying?

When Hunt had pressed Abby for the reason she wanted to pull Noah from the Club Kids program, he never imagined she would break down.

Hunt couldn't handle it when women cried. It went against his philosophy of making them happy, and made him want to turn into a giant green man and bash brick walls to protect them.

Few women had shed tears in Hunt's presence, unless they were tears of joy. But Abby was miserable. He could see it in her stiff shoulders and the look of fear in her golden eyes with traces of shadows beneath. Something or *someone* had frightened her, and damn if it didn't piss him off. Which was probably why he'd offered to set her up on the club's nonexistent scaled payment plan. And then offered to let Noah participate for free.

Levi would have his balls for that one.

Whatever. Hunt would deal with Levi later.

Noah was special to the program. He'd been here long enough to be a part of the huge expansion Club Kids had gone through over the last year or so. As far as Hunt was concerned, the club owed it to Noah to support him and his mother.

But there was more. He needed to see Noah safe. His mother as well. Which was baffling as hell.

Yes, he loved women. Yes, he wanted to protect them and make them happy. But he'd never put himself out there the way he was right now. Not since Lisa.

Nearly a cool decade had passed since he'd fallen in love with Levi's girlfriend when Hunt was only a senior in high school. After that monstrous shitstorm, Hunt hadn't had a good enough reason to be protective over anyone.

It was the kid. Hunt wanted Noah to be safe and secure, and in order to do that, Noah's mother needed support, that was all.

This was a bad idea, but he couldn't stop himself. He was going to do what he could for Noah and Abby, no matter the consequences.

Hunt stretched his neck and let out a harsh sigh while he watched Noah and his mother exit the club.

His brothers didn't think him capable of caring for someone other than himself—nor did anyone else, for that matter—but he *was* capable.

Once Abby had told him about the vise grip Noah's grandparents had on her son, Hunt had been furious. Oh, he hadn't shown it at the time, but he was *pissed*.

How dare anyone take a child from his mother? A good mother, no less. Sure, she didn't always pick up Noah on time, but it was clear she loved him. Hunt saw the way Abby looked at Noah, saw the love that glowed between boy and mother. The vision was so damned endearing that it had nearly caused him to shed a tear. *Nearly*. Let's not get crazy. Hunt had been raised by his raucous brothers;

he'd rather break a pinky finger than show that kind of emotion.

Speaking of his raucous brothers, Hunt went in search of them. They had a standing date for beers every week, typically in the Fireside Lounge at the club, but tonight they were going Mexican. Over the last few years, significant others joined them, which initially bothered Hunt. He realized now that the ladies offered better advice and were good to have around.

"You want to do what?" Levi said, his deep voice rumbling like thunder an hour later.

Hunt reached for a tortilla chip and dipped it into the extra-spicy salsa from the club's Mexican restaurant. "Free enrollment for Noah. A special exception."

Levi looked at Emily, his girlfriend and head manager at the club, as though saying, "Are you listening to this?"

"Hunt," Emily said gently, "what happened?"

Hunt chewed his chip and took a gulp of one of the restaurant's massive margaritas, complete with mini-bottles of Corona upside down on the rim. "His mom can't afford it anymore, and I think we should have a scaled payment plan." He shot a glare at his brother. "Not every kid grows up the way we did. We'd be dicks to only allow in kids who could afford our higher-than-average pricing."

Levi scratched his stubbly chin. "Fair enough. But we can't afford to give every kid *free* tuition. Scaled is one thing, but free? That wouldn't be fair to the parents who pay."

Hunt leaned back, considering. He shrugged. "I'll pay for it."

Levi looked at their brothers this time, all of whom had been quiet since Hunt had brought up Noah and his mother.

"What?" Hunt said.

Adam cleared his throat. "It's a little odd, is all. You taking such interest in a kid. Or—anyone."

Typical. People always underestimated him. Especially his brothers.

"Not odd at all," Hunt said patiently. "I enjoy hanging out with the kids at the club. Noah just happens to need my help, and I don't want to see him suffer. His mom's got shit going on with her in-laws. Well, technically not in-laws. She was never married to Noah's father, and Noah's father passed away years ago. The point is, she's a single mom doing her best, and I want to make sure she's supported— *that Noah's supported,*" he clarified.

Bran pointed. "That's the part that throws me. You've never wanted a girlfriend. Well, not since... Anyway, you haven't gotten serious about a woman in years, and now you want to take care of this mom and her kid?"

"Not take care of her. I want to help Noah." Okay, he wanted to help Abby too, but saying as much put stupid thoughts in his brothers' minds.

"Interesting," Wes said.

"What do you mean, 'interesting'?" Hunt glared and leaned back.

"Oh, nothing. Just *interesting.*"

Hunt swiped his hands down his face. Why were his brothers being so difficult? This was no big deal. "You assholes have been hounding me about my shallow hookups *for years,* and now, when I show an interest in helping out a small family in need, you're the shallow assholes. What gives?"

"Ignore them," Kaylee said, holding Harlow in her arms as the baby played with her hair. "I like it, Hunt." She looked at the others. "Noah really is a sweet kid. Everyone at Club Kids has gotten the impression things aren't easy for him at home. Now we know why. I'm all for helping him." She smiled at Hunt.

Finally. Someone with some sense.

"Plus," Kaylee said, "Noah's mom is pretty. I can see why Hunt likes her."

Hunt ground his teeth. "It's not about the mom."

"Regardless," Levi said, "we can't give the program away for free. Sets a bad precedent. And I'm not sure we wouldn't get in trouble for playing favorites if word got out."

Hunt flagged the waitress and ordered a super carne asada burrito dinner. Talking about Abby with his brothers had emotionally drained him, and now he was stress eating. Good thing he didn't gain weight. "I already told you, I'll pay. Think of it as a private donation."

"Is Noah's mom okay with that?" Kaylee asked.

Great, even his supporter was questioning him. "Not exactly. I haven't asked her. Do we have to let her know?"

Kaylee looked to Levi, who looked to Emily.

"I suppose not," Emily said carefully. "I don't think it's illegal. But it seems shifty to not tell her what you're doing. You'd be lying through omission."

Hunt twisted his mouth in thought. "I'm fine with that."

Noah needed to be at Club Kids, and his mother needed help. What kind of man would Hunt be if he didn't step up?

And if his brothers were right, and he'd never done anything like this his entire life? Well, Noah was special. Had nothing to do with Noah's mother.

Though she was pretty.

And protective of her son.

And kind of hot when she was angry and protective over her son.

But this was all about Noah.

CHAPTER EIGHT

Abby turned in her financial application to Club Kids, just to see if Hunt had been correct about the free daycare. Because, come on, he had to be wrong. And if he was wrong, then her decision was made for her and she didn't need to explain why Noah couldn't attend the program anymore. She couldn't afford it, and no one would argue with that.

Only, apparently, Club Kids *was* offering Noah free tuition.

Abby received a prompt reply notifying her that Noah's monthly tuition was covered, effective immediately.

"Covered?" This wasn't a state-run program. This was Club Tahoe's kids' program, the swankiest daycare from the swankiest resort in town. None of this made sense.

Which was why, free tuition or not, Abby didn't bring Noah back. She worried about the bullying situation and wasn't ready to jump back in. Instead, she tried a daycare closer to work. And it didn't go well at all.

"I hate this place," Noah said, as they left Mountaineers Daycare.

"Did something happen?" She scanned her son's face and arms.

"It's sooooo boring there. When can I go back to Club Kids?"

Abby's shoulders sank. For some reason, she wasn't ready to give Club Kids another try. Hunt was there, and he made her uncomfortable. Okay, that wasn't true. He made her...uneasy. Yes, uneasy, with his handsome face and muscles and willingness to solve problems. The last time she let a man solve her financial situation so she could attend school full-time, he'd died and left her alone with their young son.

She was a grown adult. Her family wasn't around, and God knew they had no money to spare. This was her life, and it was on her to solve her problems. Which meant she was responsible for making the best decisions she could for her child. "What if we stay at the Mountaineers program for a little while? You're safe there. No big kids picking on you."

"No, Mom!" Noah's sad brown eyes implored her. "I want to go back to Club Kids and help Hunt with the boats."

Crap. This was the part of parenting that sucked. You wanted to keep your kid safe, and they wanted to do something that put them in harm's way.

Though was it truly unsafe at Club Kids? Maybe they'd hired new personnel, as Hunt had promised. "I'll give them a call and see if they still have space." In other words, see if they'd hired more people before she made any decisions.

"Yay!" Noah cheered.

It struck her in the heart like a dagger to deny her son anything, when he rarely complained. In fact, returning to Club Kids was the first thing Noah had ever demanded.

And she worried it had something to do with Hunt and the bond her son had formed with him.

———

NOAH WIGGLED out of Abby's arms after she pressed a kiss to his cheek. "I'm fine," he said, and ran straight for Hunt, standing not ten feet away, checking off a list on a clipboard.

Abby had checked in with Club Kids after Noah had expressed his unhappiness at the other daycare center. Yes, they'd hired more employees. Three, in fact. And yes, they still had room for Noah.

"We'd be happy to have him back," the spunky attendant had said. Brin, if Abby was correct. So Abby had relented. Club Kids truly was the most well-respected place for childcare in town that she'd found.

Hunt glanced up, making brief eye contact with her.

A swarm of butterflies took off inside her belly.

She closed her eyes. Really? This now? Hunt had helped her with Noah and the program and, dang it, even her car. If she was going to allow him to be a friend to her and her son, she needed to keep things platonic. It was one thing for a friend to help out, and another thing entirely to have a man supporting her. She wouldn't go down that road again. Not without a wedding license.

Noah dumped his backpack and lunch in a bin set outside for that purpose, and Hunt said something to him, touching his shoulder.

Noah smiled widely then ran off to join the other kids. Hunt returned his gaze to his clipboard, but Abby sensed his attention on her.

Time to let him know where things stood. She

approached and said, "This isn't a permanent thing." He didn't look up. "Noah wants to be here, but I'm not convinced it's the best place for him. And I'll probably be late every day. I don't get out of work until five. And there's traffic. Especially in the summertime."

Hunt finally slid his gaze from the clipboard to her eyes.

Her chest tightened and her heart pounded.

She clenched her palms. Hunt hadn't had this kind of effect on her inside the club.

Okay, that was a lie. But back then she'd been in lock-down mode. She'd ignored those butterflies, and now the darn things had gotten intense.

Even if she was attracted to Hunt, she had no time to date. Like, none. Less than none. Not that he was inter-ested. The butterflies and pounding heart were probably one-way.

Hunt had never seen her in anything but her rubber work clogs. He must think her frumpy. And yeah, she was.

At one time, Abby had been an attractive woman. Back when she washed her hair daily and wore makeup and cute clothes. Now she was lucky if her nurse's smock was unwrinkled. More times than not, she was too tired to fold clothes and passed out as soon as Noah fell asleep. Being a single parent put a serious damper on the hot-mom depart-ment. Not that she needed to be hot. Abby hadn't needed to be hot since Trevor died.

"Don't worry about being late," Hunt said, his voice deep, seductive, and not at all helping. Because striking blue eyes and a built body weren't enough.

She was a single, frumpy mom, for heaven's sake! The universe needed to have pity.

"Well, I am worried," she said, lifting her chin and

trying to not look him in the eye. The butterflies tended to overreact with eye contact.

He pulled out his phone. "What's your number?"

Butterfly kaleidoscope explosion. "Excuse me?"

Bringing Noah back to Club Kids was the worst decision ever.

"Your number," he said. "I'll text you with my information. Call me if you're ever running late, and I'll tell Noah so that he doesn't worry. We'll stay busy cleaning the boat until you get here."

Hunt was killing her. And persistent. She wasn't sure she trusted him, but that was her brain speaking. Her gut was all for him.

His expression was kind. She was being overprotective of her son, but could he blame her? "Fine," she said. "Though I'm sure you have it in the paperwork."

He ran his fingers across the display as she rattled off her number, and then he tucked his phone away. "I'm sure I do. But this way I've got your permission to call you. To coordinate."

Coordinate? Why did the way he said that make her stomach flutter? On the other hand, he was helping her with her son, so she needed to simmer the hell down already.

She turned and walked away, still shaky and not at all sure she was doing the right thing. Before she left the pool area, she looked back one last time to check on Noah—and found him on Hunt's shoulders.

He carried her boy to a circle of children on the sand, and Noah laughed, raising his fist like he was king of the world.

Her throat went dry. This was what her son had been

missing. What she hadn't been able to give him. A father figure. And it seemed Noah had found one on his own.

Lord help her, why did it have to be *this* man?

CHAPTER NINE

Much to Abby's surprise, life went on like clockwork once Noah returned to Club Kids. She texted Hunt when she was running late, and Noah was always playing and having fun when she arrived. If Noah wasn't with Hunt when she picked him up, Hunt was never far away.

Noah jabbered on and on for weeks on the drive home from daycare about Hunt and all the fun things he did at Club Tahoe. There'd been no more issues with bullying, not that she blamed Club Kids anymore for the dock incident. The problem was endemic; where there were kids, there would be accidents and roughhousing. All she could do was make sure Noah was under the best adult supervision she could find, and for now, Club Kids was it. Besides, Noah was happy there.

Abby grabbed her purse from her work locker, leaving early for once, and Maria flagged her down.

"So what do you say?" she said, continuing their conversation from lunch. "It's been weeks since we went out to the club."

"I don't know," Abby said. "I'm not interested in meeting men. Not with everything that's going on with Noah's grandparents. There's not much point in mingling with the opposite sex."

Maria pulled her long, dark hair over one shoulder. "It's been four years since Trevor passed. I just think you should try getting out there again. Even if only to socialize. If more comes of it"—she shrugged—"that's a plus, right? Show Noah what a healthy relationship looks like."

Abby grabbed her keys, chuckling. Maria was laying it on thick. Her friend wanted to go out and party, but half of what she said was true. These were Abby's best years. Yet she'd give it all up to keep Noah safe. "I don't know, Maria."

Abby missed Trevor. But the sharp pain of his loss had dulled since his parents began their campaign to make things hard on her. She didn't blame Trevor for what his parents were doing, but she blamed him for not creating a will before Noah was born.

"I don't want to risk Trevor's parents throwing something else in my face to make me look like a bad parent. I'm sure if I went on a date, they'd spin it to look like I had a revolving door of men at the house."

Maria grabbed her wrists. "Abby, you didn't talk to that lawyer I referred you to, did you?"

"Sure I did. Do you know how much he charges for a one-hour consultation? That's enough for food for an entire month. I can't afford it."

"There has to be another way. The city or state must provide support for situations like this."

Abby dropped her hands from Maria's gentle grip and rubbed her forehead. "Maybe. I don't know. If Trevor's parents decide to sue me for custody, I might be able to get help. Right now, they only threaten. And it's not like I have tons of time to look into things. I'd basically be taking on a part-time job just to pay for professionals, let alone research the situation."

"All the more reason for us to get you out. We won't go to a club. We'll go someplace respectable where we can talk and think of ways to get Vivian off your back. I'm sure if we put our heads and phone-searching capabilities together, we'll come up with something."

Abby laughed. "That's how you want to spend a Saturday night?"

"Heck yeah. I'm here for you, girl. You said Vicious has Noah tomorrow night?"

"Vicious" was Maria's nickname for Vivian. "Yes. They'll probably feed him junk food all day and night so that when he comes home, he won't be able to settle down."

"That's typical grandparent behavior. You can't fault Vicious for that."

"I know, I know," Abby said, and sighed. "It's just hard to not look at everything they do as an attack."

"Which is why we'll talk it through someplace where we won't have to whisper."

"True. I don't want Noah knowing anything about what his grandparents are up to, though he's smart. I'm sure he senses the tension. I might not like what his grandparents are doing, but I want him to have a good relationship with them. Even if their main goal in life these days is to get me out of the picture."

"And on that uplifting note, is it a date? Tomorrow night?"

Abby nodded, but she wasn't so sure Trevor's parents would ever give up, no matter what ideas she and Maria came up with. Trevor's parents were extremely wealthy, with a lot of influence in Lake Tahoe and beyond. She feared she was a gazelle going up against a lion.

She didn't know what she'd do if she ever lost Noah. But she was prepared to do anything to make sure it never happened.

———

IT WASN'T until Maria pulled into the Club Tahoe parking lot that alarm bells sounded inside Abby's head. She'd been so content to not have responsibility for a few hours that she hadn't paid attention to where they were headed. "Why are we here?"

Maria put the car in park. "I thought we'd go to the Fireside Lounge. They rotate the bar menu, and this week is ground turkey apple sliders." She waggled her brows. "Island mules are the drink special."

Abby closed her eyes and slowly let out a breath. "Can we go somewhere else?"

"Why?"

Hunt, that's why.

Maria stared at her, perplexed.

"I come here every day to drop off and pick up Noah," Abby said.

"For the kids' program. But you've never come here to chill. This will be fun." Maria opened her car door and stepped out. When Abby didn't immediately exit, Maria hung her head back inside. "Don't make me drag you. Because I will. You need to get out. Even if we're not mingling socially, you so need to be among the land of the young and single."

Abby unlatched her seatbelt. She had no rational excuse, and she didn't want to give Maria the truth. Telling

Maria about Hunt—what he'd done for Abby, her unnerving attraction to him—would only give her dear friend ammunition to ask uncomfortable questions.

Club Tahoe wasn't purely a singles hangout. There were plenty of families and couples who stayed at the resort. It couldn't be that bad. Besides, what were the chances Hunt would be here? If he was a normal person, he'd run as far from Club Tahoe after work as he could get.

Apparently, Hunt wasn't normal.

As soon as they entered the Fireside Lounge, Abby caught sight of Hunt at a table with a large group of men and women in the far left corner. And there was a woman perched on Hunt's lap.

Abby's throat grew tight. He was single; of course he'd be with another woman. Many women, most likely.

As though sensing her presence, Hunt looked up and glowered.

"You're sure I can't talk you into going somewhere else?" Abby said to Maria, but it was too late. Maria was already making her way to a two-person table. Right next to Hunt and his friends.

Abby ducked her head as they walked across the room. Great. Just perfect. Why was he here? He should be at Blue Casino, drinking and hitting on women there.

How in the world would she be able to relax with Hunt staring her down? And why *was* he staring her down? He was the one with an attractive woman on his lap. The woman's chest was so close to his face that he could have turned his head and motorboated her breasts.

God, this was awful.

Abby straightened and plastered on a smile, ignoring Hunt's table as they approached the two-person table next to them. Until Maria took the seat that forced Abby to face Hunt and his friends.

She was here to get out and form a plan about Noah's grandparents. Who cared if Hunt was here too? She could ignore him and the butterflies he caused.

They ordered the famous sliders and island mules, and Abby tried to look anywhere except at the scene in front of her. The men with Hunt must be his good friends. They were laughing and having a nice time. Except, it seemed, Hunt, who hadn't lost his frown, though at least it wasn't directed at her anymore.

Now that Abby paid attention—because of course she was still looking, even if she told herself she wouldn't—she realized that one of the women at the table was the program manager from Club Kids. Abby had met Kaylee and her baby when Kaylee returned from maternity leave.

"So, I've been thinking about your problem," Maria said, breaking into Abby's thoughts of Hunt. "What if you get a roommate to help you split expenses?"

"I tried that a couple of years ago when I considered finishing my nursing degree. Have you interviewed people in this town for a roommate? It was nuts. Half of them were high on something, and the other half were too young."

"Abby, you're not even thirty."

"I realize that, but I might as well be forty-five. I'm not a partier, I don't do drugs, and I have a son to think about. There's no way I'll let anyone remotely sketchy into my house."

Maria's mouth twisted. "That does make it a challenge." She waggled her head. "I could always move out of my place—"

"No," Abby said. "You love your apartment. And you won the lottery with your roommate."

"True. But what will you do? Vicious is putting on the heat. Every week you come into work with something new she's done."

Abby dropped her head into her hands. "I don't know." A pounding at her temples increased at the mention of Vivian, a.k.a. Vicious. She raised her head to flag the waitress for a glass of water, and saw Hunt walking past their table with the woman who'd been sitting on his lap.

He was an attendant at Club Kids whom she barely knew. He was good to her son, that was true, but other than that? She shouldn't care. She really, really shouldn't care.

Maria eyed her staring at Hunt. "You know who he is, don't you?"

Abby sipped the water the waitress placed at their table. "One of the guys we met at the Blue Casino club."

"No, I mean, who he *really* is. He's a Cade, one of the richest men in town. Maybe in the state."

Abby shook her head sharply. "What are you talking about?"

"Hunt Cade. The guy you were flirting with at the Blue Casino club. He and his brothers own this place."

"Hunt *owns* Club Tahoe?" Abby's voice came out high-pitched.

"I thought you knew that the night we met him."

Abby stared at Maria in exasperation. "How would I know that? You dragged me out, because I never go out."

Maria winced. "Sorry. You're right. You've lived in isolation. Anyhoo," she said, and winked. "He's a hottie and said to be a massive player." She eyed Hunt's ass as he left the lounge with the woman. "I wouldn't mind a piece of that. In fact, I thought you were going for it. Had I known you weren't interested, I would have turned the tables. I only held back because it seemed like you two had chemistry."

"Nope, no chemistry." Lie. But no way Abby would admit the butterfly invasion when Hunt was near.

Of course Hunt was a player. He'd never acted like one with her—well, not since that first night. Since then, he'd been nothing but kind and attentive to her and Noah. "He seriously owns this place?"

Maria nodded.

That explained why he'd hang out after work. He wasn't just a daycare attendant or manager—whatever she'd assumed him to be. He had a stake in Club Tahoe's success. "Are those his brothers?"

Maria glanced behind her. "I think so. I've never met them, but they look alike, don't they? And they're hot, like Hunt." She pouted. "Taken though, from what I've heard. Except for Hunt. No woman's been able to lock him down for even a week."

Great, and this was the guy Abby's son admired.

"Hmm," Maria said.

"What is it?"

"Hunt Cade, player extraordinaire, just walked back into the lounge. Alone." She waggled her eyebrows again. "Are you sure there's no chemistry between you two?"

H unt's brothers were idiots.

"You didn't go home with her?" This from Bran, the monk. Before he met Ireland, that was. Now, he wasn't so monkish.

"What's going on?" Wes looked at his wife Kaylee. "You work with him. Is Hunt sick?"

"Not to my knowledge. Has Hunt ever turned down a woman?"

"Never," his four idiot brothers said in unison.

"Enough." Hunt rolled his eyes. "I wasn't up for it."

"You were an hour ago," Levi said. "And if I'm not mistaken, this was a woman I've seen you with before. It's because you've already had her, isn't it?"

"No," Hunt growled. Though, truth be told, he tried to avoid being with a woman more than once, and it had nothing to do with being an asshole. The opposite.

Hunt wanted women happy when they were with him. If he went out with a woman more than once, they might get the wrong idea. And that would ruin the work he'd put into making them feel good. He preferred to not ruin a good thing. Though he'd considered taking a second shot with Carrie tonight. Which was odd.

Carrie had sauntered over and sat on his lap as soon as he'd shown up to the lounge. She was smart and beautiful, and he'd considered a round two, because hey, he wasn't getting any younger.

Being around kids and families must be wearing off on him. And he'd needed a distraction from a certain club mom he couldn't stop thinking about.

Carrie had been laying it on thick, and he had a hard time turning down a lady. It went against his need to protect and please them. Typically, he made himself scarce when he saw someone from his past, but Carrie caught him unawares and his resistance depleted.

Until Abby walked in.

What was she doing here? According to her, she didn't go out. But there she was, with the same friend from the Blue Casino club.

As far as Hunt knew, Abby never came to the Fireside Lounge. It was one of his main haunts, and he'd never seen her here before. But tonight, the first night Hunt considered moving past single nights with a woman, and Abby walked in and ruined it.

He couldn't concentrate. Certainly not on the beautiful woman on his lap. His entire focus had zoned in on the woman at the table next to him with her hair pulled up in a messy bun on the top of her head, tendrils of hair that she kept tucking behind her delicate ears falling around her face.

Delicate ears?

Hunt didn't notice a woman's ears. He didn't care if they were large or small or delicate. What was the point? A woman was more than her ears. But he noticed everything about *this* woman.

Did she know what she was doing to him?

Probably not. She didn't seem aware of how pretty she actually was. Abby never dressed to impress, and he suspected she thought no one noticed her ears or eyes or toned, round ass that would fit in the palm of his hand perfectly.

Hunt frowned. He had been thinking about Abby constantly, and it was seriously pissing him off. She was a *mom*. He never dated moms. They needed more than he had to offer, and he knew his limits.

But somehow his body and mind weren't in unison. Because the next thing he knew, he stood and walked over to Abby, ignoring his brothers' whispered comments behind his back, and the logical part of his brain telling him to sit the fuck down.

"Hello," he said to Abby. He smiled at her friend. "Fancy seeing you two here."

"Another pickup line?" Abby said.

"I wouldn't dare." He pulled up a third chair and sat at their table.

"I'm Maria, by the way." Her friend leaned forward, looking over his shoulder. "Are those your brothers?"

"According to my mother," he grumbled. Typically Hunt was fine with his brothers' probing questions. He had nothing to hide. But not tonight. Tonight, his brothers were annoying as hell.

"Maria was just telling me you own Club Tahoe." Abby said it like an accusation.

"Part owner," he corrected her. "I share it with my brothers. Is there a problem?"

She pressed her soft lips together. "You could have told me."

Hunt scratched his head. What had he done wrong now? "I didn't mention it because most people already know. The place was my father's."

"Oh," Maria said, eyes sympathetic. "I heard about that. I'm so sorry for your loss."

Hunt tapped his finger on the table, staring into Abby's confused eyes. "My father died a couple of years ago. He left this place to me and my brothers."

"I'm sorry to hear that," Abby said.

He shrugged. "It was a while ago, and we weren't close."

Maria stood. "I think I'll just"—she waved toward the bar—"check on the food."

Maria left and made her way to the bar. She was giving Hunt and Abby space, and he wasn't sure how he felt about that. On the one hand, he wanted all kinds of space to be with Abby. On the other hand, he was certain it wasn't a good idea.

"But you're so good with kids..." she said.

He lifted his eyebrow. "And that means?"

"If you weren't close to your father, how are you good with kids?" She clenched her hands. "I mean... I don't mean to say..."

He decided to save her. "I want to be different than my father. Kids are important. They need attention and support."

She seemed surprised, and then she shot him a saucy look. "It's interesting you say that. I've heard your philosophy on women is quite different than the one you have for children. It appears you're allergic to romantic relationships."

"Ouch," he said, and forced a grin. It was the first time

that sort of comment stung coming from someone other than his brothers.

"Good thing I didn't let things go anywhere the night I met you," she said.

He frowned. What was that supposed to mean? "I'm a nice guy."

She huffed out a breath. "I'm sure you're a good person. And you've been kind to Noah. But nice guys commit to women they care for."

She had him spinning in circles. What was she talking about? "Maybe I haven't met the right woman?"

She waved him off and took a large gulp of her drink. The mule, if he wasn't mistaken. "That's what they all say."

He'd been called a player. Many times. But for some reason, he didn't like the implication from her. "Some guy treated you wrong, and now you hate all men?"

She glared at him, and his balls shriveled up.

Damn. Note to self: Abby had a scary evil eye.

"Why are women called man haters when they call out bad behavior from men? I don't hate men. I have a son, for goodness' sake. But men get away with too much, and women are held accountable."

"So you were treated like crap by someone."

She sighed, and her evil eye softened. "Trevor, Noah's dad, was a good guy. He never cheated on me. But he was irresponsible."

"He didn't marry you after you got pregnant."

Her shoulders tensed. "No... Yes... It was more than that. He thought he had all the time in the world to marry me, set up a trust. It turns out he didn't."

Hunt could imagine. The woman was working herself to the bone to take care of Noah. Not to mention the things she'd told him about Noah's grandparents. Noah's father hadn't thought ahead.

People probably believed Hunt irresponsible too, but they'd be wrong. If Hunt ever had a kid, he'd take care of his son, full stop. He wouldn't leave things to chance the way Noah's father had. "Don't blame all men for one man's mistake."

She rolled her eyes. "I don't think about men, let alone take the time to put blame on ones I hardly know."

"You sure about that?"

Her gaze darted to the bar, where Maria was talking to a decent-looking dude. "I should get going. Noah's grandparents canceled at the last minute, and I had to find a new sitter. I want to make sure Noah fell asleep okay."

It was early, according to Hunt's standards. And this was why he avoided moms. They had responsibilities he wasn't ready for. He'd be a good dad when the time came, but now? No way could he picture that.

Hunt lifted his chin. "You haven't even eaten your food."

Abby glanced at the bar where the food was sitting in front of Maria. "I'll take it home." She stood, and he did too. She wrung her hands. "Hunt, I appreciate you being kind to Noah, but I'd prefer it if you didn't get too close."

The fuck? "Noah's a good kid, and he's been at the club for a while. It's natural I'd know him better than the other children, but I treat him like I do all the kids."

She sent him a look.

"Well, mostly."

"If it's all the same, I don't want him getting too attached," she said. "It would hurt him if you suddenly weren't around."

He stepped closer, sensing the electricity that ignited

when he did. Sparks flying between their bodies the way they had at Blue Casino, and every other time he'd been in proximity to this woman. He'd felt none of that when Carrie was sprawled all over his lap. But Abby was a foot away and he wanted to break past the electrical current and pull her to his chest. "Where is this coming from? I'm not going anywhere."

She tucked that stubborn lock of hair behind her ear. "Maybe not. I don't know. But now that I'm aware of your reputation, I think it's best."

Anger spiked. "For whom? Noah? Or is it best for you?"

She swallowed, eyes widening. "I better go," she said, and walked around the table toward Maria.

Hunt slowly let out a breath. Not once in his life had he been so furious with a woman. Not even with Lisa. Abby was passing judgment against him before he'd done anything wrong, trying to prevent him from being close to Noah, and that just didn't sit right.

Distancing himself from Noah and Abby... He didn't like it. Not at all.

In his attempt to make every woman happy, he'd succeeded in frightening away the one woman he wanted to get closer to.

CHAPTER ELEVEN

"Where is he?" Abby searched the house, calling out her son's name, looking under tables and beds in a desperate attempt to find Noah.

The confused babysitter looked around. "I fell asleep," she said, needlessly.

Abby had returned from the Fireside Lounge and found the sitter asleep on the couch. The girl was a sound sleeper and hadn't woken when Abby arrived. It was after eleven, and she didn't blame the girl for dozing. But when she went to check on Noah, he wasn't in his bed. And that had freaked her the hell out.

Abby's heart raced, panic constricting her chest. "Where's my son?"

The young girl's eyes were so wide that they looked ready to pop out of her head. "I put him to bed hours ago. He was fine, I swear it."

Abby sank onto the couch, clutching the sides of her head, rocking back and forth. "Oh my God, oh my God." She needed to call the police. She needed to search the neighborhood. Needed to keep searching the house.

She stood and spun abruptly in a circle. She'd already checked the house. Outside... She'd search outside and call the police.

Abby grabbed a flashlight from the junk drawer and raced for the front door. There were bears in Tahoe, and other mountain creatures. She had to find Noah. *Now, now, now...*

"Your phone is ringing," the sitter said, and Abby ignored her.

She pressed her fingers to her temples. "Just grab a flashlight and help me search."

The girl pulled a flashlight from the drawer where Abby had grabbed hers. She stopped and picked up Abby's phone. "It's still ringing. Maybe it's Noah."

"Noah doesn't have a phone."

"But..."

Abby finally looked at the caller ID. It was Vivian.

If she didn't answer, Vivian would ask questions about Abby's whereabouts and assume the worst, all because she'd missed a call. She pressed to accept and flung open the front door, running down the steps. "I can't talk right now, Vivian."

"Are you missing something?"

Abby froze. "What?"

"I came by this evening to check on Noah, and that sitter you hired was so passed out on drugs that she didn't even wake. I took my grandchild to safety."

"You *what?*" Abby spun around, grabbing her head. What was wrong with this woman?

"You had no right!" Abby said. "Have you any idea how terrified I was when I got home and Noah wasn't here?"

Vivian ignored the question. "You can barely hold down a job, and now you're hiring druggies to watch my dear grandchild. I can't let this go on any longer." Vivian hung up.

Abby stared at the phone. What was that supposed to mean?

She turned to the sitter. "Why didn't you wake when I came home?"

The girl looked horrified. "My mom always says I'm a sound sleeper. I didn't hear you. I'm so sorry. Is Noah okay?"

"His grandmother walked in under your nose and took him while you slept. What if it had been a stranger?"

The girl shook her head. "But the door, it was locked. I made sure of it after you left this evening."

Abby stepped inside the house and shoved the flashlight back in the drawer. "Vivian has a key."

She pinched her eyes closed. After Trevor passed and she'd moved into a smaller place, she'd stupidly given Vivian a key, thinking it would help with Noah. She'd had no idea at the time that Vivian would use it against her.

The sitter shifted her feet. "You don't have to pay me. This is my fault."

"Are you on drugs?" Abby asked. She needed to know if there was any truth to Vivian's words, though she doubted it. Her sitter was the straight-A teenage student of one of the doctors she worked with.

"No! Never. I truly sleep like the dead. Just ask my mom."

Abby pulled money from her purse and handed it to the girl. "This isn't your fault. You locked the door. Noah's grandmother should have woken you when she walked inside."

The sitter grabbed her purse and went to the door. "I'm so sorry," she said again, and left.

Abby sank onto the couch and covered her face. Vivian had been looking for ammunition to take Noah away from Abby for years, and tonight was damning. How could Abby ever think she could have a life outside of work with someone like Vivian on her back?

Tears spilled down her cheeks. Abby was relieved that her son was okay, but she was also filled with body-freezing fear over how far Vivian was willing to go.

———

NOAH HADN'T SHOWN to Club Kids today, and Hunt learned from Kaylee that there'd been some kind of family emergency.

What emergency? Was this real, or Abby putting space between them?

He paced the dock and finally came to a decision.

This was ridiculous. Hunt would never hurt Noah. And if Abby didn't feel the chemistry Hunt did for her, he'd back off, no problem. In fact, he'd done a pretty good job of not showing his cards ever since the night at the club when she'd made it clear she wasn't interested. She had no reason to fear him, and he was going to tell her so.

Hunt asked Bran to cover the boat excursion scheduled for noon—which Bran grumbled about, but whatever—then Hunt took off for the Club Kids playroom.

Abby asked him to stay away, but he couldn't do that. He couldn't stand by and watch Noah and Abby struggle when he had the ability to help. The very least he could do was be a friend.

"Noah left his water bottle behind," Hunt told Kaylee. "I'm going to run it by their place on my way to take care of errands." Truth. Noah had left his water bottle. Not that they routinely made house calls to drop off items left behind.

Kaylee narrowed her eyes, and Harlow reached for Hunt from her mother's arms. He gave his niece a smile and kissed her small hand. "Noah can pick it up when he comes in tomorrow," Kaylee said. "There's no need for you to go out of your way."

"It's no big deal. I'm heading in that direction."

"Hunt." Kaylee gave him a knowing look. "What are you doing? I saw the way you watched Abby last night. This is more than helping out Noah."

"She's a nice woman, and she needs our support. If I'm out and about, it's easy enough for me to swing by."

Kaylee twisted her mouth. "Fine, but I'm texting her and letting her know someone from the club is dropping off Noah's water bottle. I don't want to overstep."

"Good idea." He pecked Harlow on her chubby cheek. "Catch you later."

"Hunt," Kaylee said, right as he'd turned to leave. "Be careful. She's a stressed-out mom. Please don't make things worse."

"Why would I make things worse?"

"Because you're Hunt? Lover of womankind the world over."

"Exactly." He grinned. "I'm a lover, not a fighter."

Kaylee sighed. "Please don't get involved with one of our clients. The club is just starting to pick up business with you and your brothers in charge. Don't ruin it for the family."

"Ye of little faith." He shook his head, his expression light, but the comment stung. His family didn't believe in him. At all. They thought him a careless ass.

He wasn't careless. An ass? Yeah, okay, sometimes.

When his brothers were involved. But when it came time to man up, he was there. He'd just not had the opportunity of late. Like, say, in the last ten years or so.

But something told Hunt that if there was anyone he needed to man up for, it was Abby and Noah.

CHAPTER TWELVE

Hunt checked the address he'd grabbed from the Club Kids computer, and stared at the small cabin set between two apartment buildings. Basically, one of the seedier locations in town, with high renter turnover and close to the casinos.

He stepped out of his Range Rover and tucked Noah's water bottle in the back pocket of his jeans. The location was fairly quiet, with pines filling in the space between buildings, but damn, her place was small. No garage or carport, just a square structure that couldn't have more than one bedroom, with a roof that pitched forward and had chipped exterior paint.

Hunt jogged up the steps, a plastic pot of colorful red and purple flowers on the stoop. Set there to cheer up a sketchy cabin?

He knocked on the door and waited. He was just about to knock again when the door opened slowly.

Abby peered out, dark circles under her eyes, her long, wavy hair hanging around her shoulders. She wasn't wearing scrubs for once. Instead she had on a loose T-shirt and jeans. "Hunt?"

"Hi. Did you get the message from Kaylee?"

"Message?" Abby looked dazed. She opened the door wider and walked inside.

Hunt hesitated for a moment then stepped in behind her.

She wandered to a small kitchen counter and picked up her phone. "I haven't checked my messages in the last hour." She flipped through screens. "You didn't have to come all this way to drop off Noah's water bottle." Her voice caught on Noah's name, and Hunt frowned.

"Is everything okay?" he asked.

Clearly not. Her gaze was glassy, her eyes red as though she'd been crying. But this was why he'd come. He'd worried when Noah hadn't shown.

Noah was often the first to arrive at the club, and the last to leave. As long as Noah had been coming to Club Kids, Hunt hadn't seen the boy sick once. Something was off. "Where's Noah?"

Abby squeezed her eyes shut, and that was when the dam broke. She covered her face and her shoulders jerked in spasms. She crossed to the couch and sank down. "Gone."

Hunt sat beside her, his expression tight. "Gone where?" She wouldn't show her face, and Hunt gently pulled her hands away to see her eyes. "What's happened?"

Abby brushed tears from her cheeks. "Saturday night, Noah's grandmother came by while I was at the Fireside Lounge. She took him."

"Took him? Took him where?"

She stared down. "Vivian, Noah's grandmother, called

Child Protective Services and claimed I'd gone out to party and left my son with inadequate supervision."

"What?" Hunt roared.

She bit her lip. "Vivian has a key to my place. She came in while the sitter was sleeping and took Noah. Vivian called CPS and told them that I let a drug addict watch my child. It's not the first time she's called them when she thought she had something against me. And now CPS is investigating. I can't get Noah back from Vivian until I go through the proper procedures and prove that I can keep him safe."

Hunt dragged a hand through his hair. "What's the deal with the grandmother?"

"She's obsessed with gaining custody of Noah. She won't stop." Abby's face contorted in pain. "I don't know what to do. I've tried to be perfect. To provide for my son. But I can't fight Trevor's parents. They have too much money. Too many resources."

What kind of grandparents would take a child from his mother? And a good mother at that, not some parent who didn't give a shit.

Abby looked at him, her gaze intent. "I have to get him back."

"You'll get him back." Already, Hunt's mind worked, running through the options.

A knock sounded at the front door, and Abby jerked.

"You expecting someone?" Hunt asked.

"No. I wasn't even expecting you."

She stood and walked to the door, opening it hesitantly the way she had when he'd arrived. "Vivian?"

The grandmother? Hunt stood, his protective reflexes going into overdrive. *Keep calm*, he told himself.

"Hello, Abby." Vivian looked past Abby to Hunt, and

her eyes narrowed. "I see you have company." Her tone was mocking.

Fuck that. Hunt walked over and stood beside Abby.

"May I come in?" Vivian asked.

"How is Noah?" Abby said, opening the door wider so Noah's grandmother could enter.

"He's flourishing. He loves spending time with me and his grandfather."

"What have you told him?" Abby asked. "About why he's staying with you?"

"Don't worry," Vivian said. "I haven't mentioned anything about your inability to keep him safe. Yet."

Abby clenched her hands. "Vivian, please don't do this. I love my son. There's nothing I want more than to take good care of him and raise him in a way that would make Trevor proud."

Vivian looked past her and stared at Hunt. "How can you do that when you're out gallivanting around with men? I'm certain Trevor wouldn't approve."

"I rarely go out."

"She has no need to," Hunt cut in.

Abby sent him a weary glance.

She needed him. And he was willing to step up for her.

"Oh?" Vivian said. "And who are you?"

Abby started to reply, but Hunt spoke before she could answer.

"Her fiancé."

CHAPTER THIRTEEN

Abby's gaze shot to Hunt, her eyes wide.

"Fiancé?" Vivian said, and looked at Abby. "My, you *have* been busy."

Abby rubbed her face. "It's not like that."

"Why did you come here?" Hunt asked.

Vivian sneered, then schooled her expression. "To grab my grandson's favorite blanket. He seems to have trouble sleeping without it."

Abby's back stiffened. "He's not okay? You told me he was fine."

Vivian waved her off. "He's fine. Just has a little trouble settling down at night."

Abby began to pace.

Hunt put a hand on her arm and pulled her aside. "Grab his blanket and get Vivian to leave," he whispered.

"What are you doing, telling her you're my fiancé?" she said. "You have no idea what you've just done. Vivian will use it against me."

"Let her try."

"Hunt," she said, and groaned.

He rested both hands on her slight shoulders. She wasn't short, but she was a lot smaller than him. "Listen to me. I'm not going to let this woman take Noah from you. Will you trust me?"

"I barely know you," she said flatly.

"But I know Noah. And you know I'll do anything to keep him safe."

She paused. A long pause as she stared into his eyes. Then she nodded.

And really, what choice did Abby have? Noah's grandparents were pulling out the big guns to take custody. Abby needed support. Support he could offer. "Grab Noah's things. I'll watch the grandmother."

Abby rolled her eyes. "She's not going to rob the place."

"No." He glanced toward the front door where Vivian stood. "But she's wily. I don't trust her. Do you?"

"Good point. Just don't say anything else that might make the situation worse."

He grinned. "Would I ever do that?"

"Yes."

"You said you'd trust me."

"Only because I'm desperate," she said.

"I'm fine with that. In any case, I've got your back." He gave her a light shove in the direction of a hallway. "Be quick."

As soon as Abby entered one of three doors down the hall, Vivian reeled toward Hunt. "Fiancé, you said? How long has this been going on?"

"It's recent." *Truth.* "But I've known your grandson for a year, and I plan to take care of him and his mother."

Vivian chuckled. "She's losing custody of her son, if you haven't heard. She has no idea how to properly care for my grandchild."

Hunt doubted Abby was losing custody of Noah, and he knew damn well that Abby was a good caregiver.

His blood pressure rose, and he took a calming breath. No sense in getting into it with this woman. Not now. He had to do this the right way for Abby and Noah's sake.

Abby returned holding a blanket and a few other items. She handed them carefully to Vivian. "Will you tell Noah that I'll call him tonight?"

Vivian pursed her lips. "If you feel it's necessary."

"She's his mother," Hunt said. "It's necessary."

Vivian studied him. "I'm not sure CPS would agree."

Hunt opened the door and stepped aside for Vivian to exit. "You'll be hearing from our lawyer regarding the false accusations you've made against my fiancée."

Vivian's mouth parted, and then her face hardened. "We'll see about that." She stepped outside and quickly made her way to a brand-new Lexus.

Hunt shut the door, letting out a deep breath.

Abby punched him in the shoulder. "What are you doing?"

He rubbed his arm. "Getting Noah back?"

"By lying to his grandmother? Don't you think she'll find out we're not actually getting married?"

Hunt walked to the couch and sat. "Hear me out."

She followed him and sat as well, but she put two feet of space between them. "I don't need this kind of trouble, Hunt."

"But what if it's not trouble? If we get married, you have my name and influence in this town to back you up."

"Have you lost your mind? The fiancé bit I could understand to get Vivian to leave, but actual marriage? It isn't going to get my son back. Not if Vivian finds out we're lying.

And you've already admitted you have a loose background with women."

Damn, that was a valid point. "Even players settle down."

"Are you seriously telling me you want to marry me to help with Noah?"

"Yes." And also because he wanted to help Abby. He was drawn to her, and being married didn't sound so foreign when he thought about it with Abby.

She stared at him for what felt like twenty minutes, but was probably more like two. "I need to think about it."

"Think quickly. I want to hire a lawyer, and if we're engaged, my involvement in any custody issues with Noah will make more sense."

Abby rubbed her forehead. "I can't afford a lawyer."

"Maybe not, but I can."

She closed her eyes. "What in God's name are you getting out of this?"

"Nothing on the surface, except to help out a mother and a kid I care about."

"Me? You care about me?"

He nodded.

He wasn't sure what it was about Abby—maybe a little bit of everything—but Hunt was drawn to her in a way he hadn't been to any woman. He'd not thought to go to this length to help her and Noah, but once he'd met the she-devil, Vivian, he realized they needed him. It was wrong what the grandmother was doing, and Hunt had the resources to stop it.

"We can keep it a marriage in name only." Hunt would like more with Abby, but he'd never push it. However, should things happen naturally...who was he to fight nature?

"What happens when you go out with other women?"

He shrugged. "I won't."

She looked at him like he was crazy. "You're willing to give up women, pay for a lawyer, and get married, just to help me?"

He didn't want to think about how far he was willing to go to protect Abby and Noah, because he couldn't explain it. "Yes. Until you get your son back and have the custody squared away. I'll also make sure you and Noah are set up. My brothers and I inherited money from our father. I've been meaning to do something with it."

She laughed and shook her head in disbelief. "You have money burning a hole in your pocket, and this is what you do with it?"

It did sound crazy, but if he couldn't explain his need to help Abby to himself, he certainly couldn't explain it to her. "Look, there's plenty in my account for me to help you and Noah, and a dozen other families. We'll sign a prenup, if it will make you feel better."

"Except that we won't sleep together or consummate the marriage."

Hunt let out a choke. Truth be told, he'd like to consummate the marriage. Shit, he'd like to consummate the engagement. But he wanted Noah and Abby safe more. "Right. If that's what you want."

Her eyes narrowed. "This isn't some kind of strategy to get me into bed, is it?"

He grinned cockily. "I've never had to marry a woman to get her into bed."

She bit her lip. "That's probably true. Still, I need to think about it. You can't expect me to immediately agree to this scheme. It's totally nuts, you know."

Again, he shrugged. "Makes sense to me, but sure, take

your time." He rose and walked to the door. "But just so you know, as soon as you give me the word, I'm going to hire the best family lawyer in town. I want to get Noah out of that woman's clutches."

Abby's chest shook and tears fell from her eyes. She nodded. "Thank you. For today. And for considering ways to help me."

Consider it? His mind was already made up. Now he just needed to convince Abby.

CHAPTER FOURTEEN

Maria choked on a sip of white wine. "He what?"

"Keep your voice down." Abby glanced across the room at Noah playing a game on Maria's computer. "Hunt asked me to marry him," she said quietly.

Maria's gaze shot to Abby's ring finger.

"It's not like that," Abby said. "It wouldn't be real. It would be a marriage in name only. Something to show I'm in a stable situation, and hopefully get Vivian off my back."

"A marriage of convenience," Maria said.

"Yes." And wow, did that sound wrong. Was Abby seriously considering it?

"Does Vicious know you're marrying this guy?" Maria asked.

Abby winced. "I haven't agreed to marry him, and that's the tricky part. He called himself my fiancé right in front of her. He was trying to help, but it does put me in a bind. I don't know why he offered or why he would go to this length to help out Noah and me."

Maria set her glass on the dining table. "Honestly? I don't know either. This isn't meshing with the Hunt Cade

I've heard about. That man is a love god. Have you any idea how many women he's slept with?"

"Eww, no. And please don't tell me. I'm struggling with the proposal. I don't need numbers like that affecting my ability to make a sound decision.

"Society might view me as a better provider if I'm married—not that it's right, but that's the way the world works. As long as I don't marry a psychopath." She searched her friend's eyes. "Can I trust Hunt? Or is this the worst idea ever?"

Maria took in a deep breath, then made a funny, screwed-up face and let it out. "It could be your *best* idea. Or Hunt's best idea, since he was the one to come up with it. If it makes any difference, nothing alarming comes to mind, and you know I'll tell you if I think you're making a mistake."

Abby chuckled. "You have a very loose filter."

"Why, thank you." Maria said.

"Seriously, though, Maria, I can't screw this up. CPS ordered Vivian to return Noah to me, because there wasn't evidence of wrongdoing, but what about the next time Noah's grandparents try something? What if I marry Hunt, and he's not the man I think he is? It could make things worse."

Maria looked away absently. "Hard to imagine things could get worse, what with the slander campaign Vicious is unleashing. Hunt would have to do something truly irresponsible. Or suddenly turn into a violent man. And I've never heard anything about the Cades being violent. Well" —she snorted—"there was that time at his brother's engagement party...but does that count?"

"Yes!"

Maria waved her off. "Brothers and fisticuffs go hand in

hand. According to all reports, it was a hell of a party, and the hot-man scuffle was the icing on the cake."

Abby rubbed her head. "Oh my God, you're as crazy as Hunt."

"Crazy smart?" Maria said. "Why yes, I am. So you'd be silly to turn down Hunt's offer. Now, let's get to the important stuff. Exactly what kind of marriage is this going to be, hmm?"

Abby rolled her eyes. "In name only, remember? Prenup and all."

Maria's eyes narrowed. "You sure you can stick to that agreement?"

"The prenup?" Abby said. "Of course."

Maria shoved her shoulder. "You know what I mean. The *other* stuff. The hot sexy-time stuff."

Abby's head swung around to where Noah sat, but he was laughing at a cartoon hopping across the computer screen. "Keep. It. Down." She death-glared her friend.

"Answer the question."

"Hunt said he wouldn't date other women while we are married."

"Really?" Maria's brow rose. "Wow. Okay, well, that still doesn't answer my question. What about you, the wifey?"

Abby cleared her throat, which suddenly felt dry. "We'll keep things platonic."

Maria lifted a finger. "Let me get this straight. You'll be married to one of the hottest men in town...and not touch him?"

Abby coughed into her hand. It sounded ludicrous, when Maria put it like that. "Yes, that's right."

Maria slammed her palm on the table and Abby jumped. "You're going to be in a damned sexual vortex,"

Maria whispered, finally keeping her voice down with Noah only a few feet away. "He'll be hot and bothered and without an outlet, and so will you. There's no way two beautiful people, who are attracted to each other, wouldn't lose their minds in that situation."

"I don't really think he's—"

"Knock it off," Maria said sharply. "He's attracted to you. I saw him with you at the club and then at the Fireside Lounge, remember?"

Abby's radar was skewed, what with her celibate lifestyle since Trevor's passing. She'd wondered if Hunt was attracted to her, but he'd done such a good job keeping his distance when she discouraged his initial advances that she didn't know anymore.

Maria screwed up her face again, but this time, there was a glint in her eye. "Are you sure he's going to abstain from sex? Because that doesn't sound like the guy around town everyone's known him to be. I might have to come in and rescue him."

Abby chuckled. "Are you planning on helping him out with his dry spell?"

"Well," Maria said, and sat back all casual, "I am nothing if not a good friend."

Maria was kidding. Well, half kidding. "He's handsome and there will be temptation." Maria made a face. "Fine," Abby said. "I've considered what he looks like without his clothes on."

Maria nodded. "That's what I'm talking about."

"But this isn't about me and my dating life," Abby said. "I have to keep things platonic. What if we crossed that line and it didn't work out? Then I'd be a *divorced* single mother. Lord only knows what Vivian would do with that information. She'd find some way to use it against me like she has everything else."

Maria slowly nodded. "Right. Like the vaccinations."

Abby threw up her hands. "Those stupid vaccinations. I only wanted to draw out the schedule, not send Noah to school unvaccinated. But Vivian remembered when he was three that he still wasn't totally caught up, and she used it against me. I have no idea who Vivian told inside the education department, but whoever it was nearly blackballed my child. I'm still going around town showing people in the district that Noah's up to date. I swear that woman looks for any reason to paint me as a bad mother."

Maria nodded. "She does... Okay, so fine, a marriage in *name only*—God help you. The question is, will you go through with it?"

Abby slowly sucked in a breath. "I'm tempted. I don't know if Vivian could actually take Noah away from me, but that woman is crazy. And powerful with all the money they have. I don't want to take any chances with her. *I can't.*"

"You could always move away," Maria said.

Abby sighed. "I've thought about it. But Noah loves Lake Tahoe, and it's the last part he has of his father. I also strongly sense that Vivian's reach would extend any distance. In fact, I wouldn't put it past her to file some sort of lawsuit to prevent me from moving Noah away. And without money, I can't fight."

"Moving isn't cheap, either," Maria said, her mouth twisted in thought.

"There's something else," Abby said. "Before I came over today, I maybe sort of cyber-stalked Hunt."

"Of course you did." Maria leaned forward and grinned. "What did you find out?"

"His worst crime seems to be his love for women, like

you said. There are pictures of him all over women's Instagram and Facebook accounts, though he doesn't appear to have any accounts of his own." She shrugged, frowning. "I guess I could turn the other shoulder if he changes his mind about not seeing women while we're married."

Abby's stomach soured. Even if they married, she'd have no claim on Hunt. But the idea of him with someone else while they lived together was just—gah, not right either.

"It's like you told me," Abby said. "The man is sex on a stick. Why wouldn't he cave to some woman hitting on him?"

"Because he said he's willing to make a commitment to you?" Maria pointed out. "He's a player, but unlike most players, I swear that man has the most beloved reputation among women. That wouldn't be the case if he were a dick. He doesn't lie and screw women over, he just...doesn't commit."

"Yet he's committing to me?"

"Yes." Maria nodded slowly, her expression serious. "Think about that. You're a catch when you're not stressed out with work and life. Maybe he genuinely likes you? Maybe he genuinely wants to help?"

Abby closed her eyes. "And we're back to square one. That this could be the right thing to do for Noah and me."

"You should marry him," Maria said.

Abby blinked. "Really?" She had been considering going through with it, and now her best friend in town was telling her to do it too.

"He and his brothers are bazillionaires," Maria said, "and money builds power. Let me put it to you this way; those brothers have more money and influence than Vicious, and that's key. If Hunt is sincere—and from what you've said, I believe he is—he'll hold up his end of the bargain."

Abby rubbed her forehead and glanced at Noah. "I can't pass it up, can I?"

Maria pushed Abby's full glass of wine closer. "Not if you're smart."

CHAPTER FIFTEEN

I t was Monday and Abby had it off, so she'd kept Noah out of Club Kids for the day. She planned to play with him and get housework done. She'd love to skip the house-work portion, but Noah was out of underwear and Abby didn't even want to consider what kind of negligence Vivian would claim over that one. Besides, Abby was out of clean scrubs, so it was all-around dire straits in the laundry department.

"What do you feel like for breakfast? Waffles or pancakes?" she asked Noah.

He rubbed his eyes, wearing pajama bottoms and a T-shirt. He'd just emerged from his bedroom after sleeping in until eight, thank the universe. "Pancakes with extra syrup," he said in a sweet, groggy voice, and flung himself face-first onto the couch.

"You got it." Abby was more optimistic this morning than she'd been in a long time. She didn't feel so backed to the wall. Abby had options. True, they involved a man she barely knew, but Hunt was offering a tempting alternative to the daily struggle she'd met for years.

She scrolled until she found an old playlist with Aretha Franklin's "Respect" on it and cranked up her phone, swinging her hips as she prepped the pancake batter.

Giggles ensued from behind the counter, and she glanced over her shoulder.

"You're funny, Mommy." Noah was grinning, his knees tucked up near his chin. "Why are you dancing?"

"Because we're going to eat pancakes and Aretha is playing." She lifted the stirring spoon to her mouth like a microphone and lip-synced the chorus.

Noah jumped up and jerked his narrow hips while hopping around the living room. "R, E, S, Peee, C, P," he shouted.

Abby laughed at her son's slaughter of the lyrics. "You've got moves, little man. Just wait until the girls see how well you dance. They won't know what hit them."

Noah jumped onto the couch and shook his hips to the beat, kicking his leg in the air in a karate move.

Laughing, Abby turned and carefully poured the batter onto the grill she'd preheated. She set the bowl down and spun just in time for the next chorus, with a spoon to her mouth, eyes closed for emphasis.

Only, when she opened her eyes, Noah wasn't alone.

"Gah!" Abby yelled, and stumbled back.

Hunt stood across the counter from her, arms crossed, feet spread apart. He quirked his eyebrow.

Noah stood next to him in an identical posture. Only he was unable to keep a straight face.

Abby set the spoon on the counter and quickly wiped her hands on a dishtowel. "What are you doing here?"

"Big Aretha fan, eh?" Hunt asked.

Noah dropped to the floor in a fit of giggles.

She frowned at her son then looked back at Hunt. "Do you always walk into people's homes unannounced?"

Hunt stepped toward the front door and appeared to be checking the doorknob and lock. "Came by to fit the front and back doors with a chain lock. I noticed there wasn't one the last time I was here." He finished his inspection and looked back. "I would suggest you change the locks so that *certain people* with access can't just walk in whenever they feel like it." He sent her a knowing look.

Vivian, she thought, remembering how she'd told Hunt that she'd stupidly given Vivian a key to her home years ago.

"But I don't think your landlord would appreciate that," he said, and looked past her toward the stovetop. "I called," he said, seemingly distracted by the food. "And knocked. Your performance must have muffled the sound. You don't check your phone very often, do you?"

Busted.

"Besides," he said, "once Noah started shouting about PCP and drugs, I thought I should check in on things and make sure everything was okay. Your door was unlocked, by the way."

She twisted her mouth in annoyance. "First of all, I'm home. Sometimes I leave the door unlocked during the day. Second, Noah's five. He got the lyrics wrong. And getting back to your purpose here, I can't install a chain on my door. My landlord wouldn't like that any better than changing the locks."

He scratched the side of his jaw, scruffy as though he'd run out in a hurry this morning and hadn't taken the time to shave. "It's nothing permanent. They'll probably appreciate the extra security. Everyone wants their property protected." He notched up his chin. "What're you cooking over there? Looks like pancakes."

"That's because it is pancakes." Speaking of—Abby spun to flip the food before it burned. Hunt was rubbing his stomach when she turned back around.

"I haven't eaten breakfast myself." He gave her the saddest puppy-dog eyes she'd ever seen. "I wanted to run this errand before I went into work."

She shook her head. "That's the most pathetic attempt at inviting yourself to breakfast."

"Did it work?" He lowered his voice. "Besides, I'm doing my *fiancé* duties and taking care of my woman. Can't have the doors unsecured. What kind of man would I be if I put my food intake ahead of your and Noah's safety?"

Her belly dropped. Damn him, he was good.

But that wasn't what this was about. It was all a show. Only now, Noah was an avid audience to the interplay between her and Hunt.

"What's a fiancé?" Noah asked.

If Abby followed through with the fake marriage, Noah would need to see this. He'd need to know Abby and Hunt were more than just friends. She hated lying to her son, but she couldn't tell him the truth until she'd made a firm decision. Noah was completely guileless at this age, and incapable of lying. Vivian would hear the truth from Noah, and the jig would be up.

"I'll explain later," she told Noah. She sent Hunt a look. "Would you like to join us for breakfast?"

He gave her a toothy grin. "Only if it's not too much trouble."

AFTER A BREAKFAST in which both boy and man consumed an inordinate amount of pancakes and bacon, Abby stood and put dishes in the dishwasher.

"I have a proposition for you," Hunt said, and Abby looked up. "What do you think of me taking Noah to the store to buy those chain locks? You'd have an hour or so to yourself."

An entire hour to herself? Yes, there was laundry to do, but still... Except this wasn't Club Kids. This was Hunt taking her son in the car and driving off somewhere. "I don't know," she said, and looked at Noah.

"Yes!" Noah shouted, and ran to his bedroom.

Hunt laughed. "Sorry, I shouldn't have said it in front of him. You can still back out."

If she was considering marrying this man, she needed to be able to trust him around her son. Technically, Hunt spent as much time with Noah as she did—or more so due to Club Tahoe—so it was silly to stand on ceremony now.

Noah returned and stripped off his pajamas before putting on pants and a T-shirt. The shirt went on backward, of course.

Abby closed her eyes and pinched the bridge of her nose. "Noah, we change in the bedroom."

"Hunt's leaving," Noah said, "and I want to go with him."

Hunt looked up, a question on his face.

There went her quality time with her son on her day off. Truthfully, she spent almost no time by herself, and she could use it. "Okay, but can you take my car? It has the car seat."

Hunt looked out the window and winced. "No, no, I got this."

She put her hands on her hips. "Is Sunflower not good enough for you?"

"Sunflower?"

"My car is delicate. The name fits her."

Hunt chuckled. "Delicate is one way of putting it. I'm afraid I won't actually make it to work today if I attempt to drive Sunflower to the store and back."

She wanted to be insulted, but no joke, it could happen. "You can't drive Noah without a car seat."

"Which is why I'll take yours from Sunflower and install it in my car."

"You know how?"

He sent her an incredulous look. "I have a niece. I know how to install a car seat."

"Interesting." And it *was* interesting to think of Hunt taking his niece around town. And pretty darn cute. "Well," she said, "it's less of a car seat and more of a booster, since Noah's older now. Should be easy to install."

"No worries." He looked out the window again. "What do you say about me taking Noah across the street to that park? If I know him"—Hunt winked at her son—"your boy needs to get a few wiggles out after eating all those pancakes."

This was almost like having a babysitter. Hunt was good with kids. Really good. And he paid attention.

She looked at Noah, who was jumping up and down and tugging on Hunt's arm. "I guess that's a yes," she said.

"Be back in a few." Hunt walked out the door with Noah.

Abby watched them from the living room window, and saw Hunt hold Noah's hand and look both ways before they crossed the street.

Even Noah's father hadn't been as conscientious with

their son as Hunt had been just now. Abby didn't realize until Trevor was gone how much she'd looked after things on behalf of the both of them.

Whatever this was between her and Hunt, it was temporary. She didn't want to get used to the help, because she'd sorely miss it when it was gone.

Abby should have been folding laundry or finishing those dishes she'd started, but she couldn't take her eyes off Hunt and Noah playing in the park.

Currently, Noah had his arms and legs wrapped around Hunt's torso like a spider monkey, while Hunt did pull-ups on one of the tall playground bars.

Noah wasn't light at over forty pounds, and Hunt was doing pull-ups with the extra weight like it was nothing. How did he do it?

Hunt's biceps bulged with each repetition, his body tight and angled to support Noah on his chest. It was mesmerizing.

Until Noah began to slip.

Abby yelped, hand flying to her mouth.

But Hunt smoothly dropped to the ground, his arm already secured around Noah. He was in perfect control, this strong man with her son.

Her eyes grew wet, nose burning. She would not cry. That was ridiculous. It was only that she'd never seen a man so thoroughly careful and kind to Noah. Trevor had been a loving father, but he'd always put his me-time first. The birth of their child hadn't slowed Trevor's outdoor adventures one bit.

Noah ran to the slide, and Hunt followed him. They played on the equipment for a few more minutes, with Hunt pushing Noah on the swing or catching Noah when he flung himself at Hunt from atop the playground set. And then they were walking back toward the house.

Abby sucked in a breath and rushed for a tissue to blow her nose. She quickly grabbed the laundry basket and began folding clothes. She smiled when they walked in the door. "How was it?"

"Great!" Noah said.

Hunt hadn't even broken a sweat; the clean scent of his soap wafted past her on his way to the kitchen counter. "You mind if I grab your car keys? I'll get that booster seat set up, and we can be on our way."

"Sure." Abby strode across the room and fished inside her purse for her keys. She handed them to Hunt.

"Thanks," he said. "Be right back."

Abby looked down at Noah. "Use the bathroom before you leave, okay?"

Noah raced to the bathroom, did his business, splashed water on his hands for less than half a second, then ran back out.

She'd never seen her son so excited to spend time with someone. She had a special bond with Noah, but it was clear he'd been missing a man in his life.

Hunt returned, and Noah was already racing past her to buckle himself in the shiny new Range Rover.

Of course Hunt wouldn't want to drive Sunflower when he had *that* beauty. Not that Sunflower wasn't pretty. She was just...special.

Fine, her car sucked.

"Okay, so you'll call me if you need anything?"

He sent her a knowing look. "We'll be fine. Enjoy your free time. And try not to spend it all on chores. If I return and those dishes are gone from the sink, I won't be happy." He winked.

"Hunt," Abby said. She'd already made her decision. It had come to her sometime between the pull-ups and the slide. "The answer is yes. To your question. I'll—marry you," she said quietly, though Noah was nowhere near earshot.

Hunt blinked, and then a smile slowly spread across his face. "It's going to work out. You'll see." Before she could gather her wits, he was out the door and headed for his car.

Abby collapsed on the couch, shivers racking her body. "Holy shit."

Had she really agreed to this? And if it was a marriage in name only, how would she fight her attraction to the handsome man in her house?

CHAPTER SIXTEEN

"Getting married? As in *married*, married?" Levi made a practice swing with his golf club like he was swinging a baseball bat, ready to blast the ball into outer space. Emily thought her boyfriend was soft on the inside, but Hunt never saw that side of Levi. He was all brute force.

Hunt furrowed his brow and set his golf bag down. "Is there some other form of marriage I'm not aware of?"

Levi glanced at their brothers standing around the first tee holding similar expressions of disbelief. He dropped the head of his driver on the tee box and leaned on the handle. "Leave it to you to do things ass-backwards. This isn't some game, Hunt. We're talking about a single mother and her son you'll be responsible for."

Hunt looked up and slowly let out a strained breath. "I'm aware of that. I'm not some impulsive eighteen-year-old."

Levi chopped his hand through the air. "You're always playing with the kids at the club—"

"Because it's my job! You should try it sometime. It's cathartic."

"—and you go out almost every night looking for hookups."

Don't have to look, Hunt thought but didn't say. "I'm capable of commitment."

"Oh really?" Levi said, again turning to their brothers for backup. *Dammit.*

So Hunt hadn't committed since the disaster with Lisa nearly ten years ago, but still. "I don't need hookups. They simply kill time."

Wes bounced Harlow in the BabyBjörn she'd nearly outgrown. But they couldn't let her loose on the course. That one was a runner. "There's no reason to believe Hunt will mess this one up," Wes said.

"Thanks." Hunt rolled his eyes. Did none of them have faith?

"No, really," Wes continued, taking a practice swing one-handed. He couldn't do it with both hands without jostling Harlow. "You're great with the kids at Club Kids. Kaylee says so all the time."

Levi glared at Wes. "And that's supposed to make him a family man?"

Wes shrugged, then ducked at the sound of someone yelling, "Fore!" from a mile away.

Hunt looked up, but the ball landed nowhere near them.

Crouched and blocking Harlow, who already wore a specially designed baby golf helmet, Wes said, "None of us were raised to be family men. That doesn't mean we can't adapt." Wes gestured to himself.

True, Wes had shocked them with his dad skills. And

they couldn't fault him for his overprotectiveness of Harlow, because they all behaved that way around her.

Harlow swung a short plastic golf club and smacked her father in the head.

"Good job, Harlow," Wes cooed, and kissed her on the cheek.

Bran walked up to the tee and took a practice swing. "As much as I enjoy these family discussions, I gotta get back to the restaurants. If we're going to play, let's play." He shot a look at Levi. "You can't control who Hunt marries."

The only brother missing from this diatribe was Adam, and only because he was running late.

Levi's expression didn't change. *Shit.* Hunt wasn't going to like what his brother said next. "You're the most fucked up of all of us. Maybe it's because you never knew Mom. Never had that maternal influence in your life. I'm not sure why you are the way you are, but I don't want to see you hurt that woman and her child."

Hunt's blood rushed through his veins and his head pounded. "I will *never* hurt Noah and Abby. I'm doing this for them, you idiot. And if I'm scarred, so are the rest of you. We all lost Mom and Dad when Mom died."

Hunt scrubbed a rough hand down his face. He knew what this was about. He'd always known what Levi thought. Not like his brother hid it. "Just admit it. You don't trust me."

No answer.

"Fuck you, Levi." Hunt grabbed his clubs and stormed off the course, leaving his brothers gaping.

He never showed Levi how much his shit got to him. Okay, almost never. But this was different. Hunt had never been as serious as he was when it came to Noah and Abby. And he didn't know how to explain his feelings to his brothers—or to himself, really. He just felt an overpowering instinct to protect them. And as long as Abby was willing, that was what he would do.

Hunt thought if he could get Levi's support, his other brothers would follow suit at the news of his sudden engagement. But the conversation hadn't gone as planned. None of them supported Hunt, with maybe the exception of Wes, who was the kind of father none of them expected him to be.

But Hunt didn't need his brothers. If he had to, he'd marry Abby at the courthouse without any of them. This wasn't about his brothers, anyway. Hunt would keep Noah and Abby safe if it was the last thing he did.

———

ONE WEEK LATER, Hunt stood inside the small, rustic Fallen Leaf Lake chapel alongside Abby. A manager friend at the lake's general store had gotten them a chapel slot despite the short notice. Hunt wore a new suit just for the occasion. He could have worn one he already owned, but it seemed only right to buy new clothes on his wedding day. Given his track record, this might be his one and only.

Abby had told Noah they were getting hitched a few days ago, and the little guy had been attached to Hunt's side the rest of the week whenever Hunt worked at Club Kids.

A smile pulled at Hunt's lips. He loved the idea of having Noah for a son. Even if it was short term.

His smile fell. His marriage to Abby was temporary. Just long enough to protect Noah and Abby from Noah's grandparents, and to provide them with a stable home. But that would take time, wouldn't it? Not like they could show a united front in just a couple of months; the grandparents would never believe it.

Hunt's shoulders loosened, and he looked down at the woman holding on to his left arm. Abby wore a white, ankle-length sundress, her hair pulled up with a few wisps of artfully messy curls falling around her forehead and neck. If Hunt envisioned the perfect bride, he couldn't do better than Abby. The more time he spent with her, the more beautiful she became to him.

A light bump hit Hunt from behind, and a sweaty hand grabbed his right palm.

He smiled down at Noah, who must have gotten bored standing as his best man and decided to join the party.

Noah wore a matching suit. Couldn't let the kid wear jeans to his mother's wedding, could he? Abby had been surprised when Hunt suggested he buy Noah an outfit for the wedding, but she'd smiled shyly and allowed it.

The rest of the last week, Hunt had been busy talking with lawyers and arranging the wedding, the details of which Abby had been all too happy to hand off. She had work, and Hunt's schedule was flexible. Meaning he forced his brothers to cover for him when he had an appointment. He'd also quickly gotten a prenup drawn up, following through on his promise to Abby when he'd been trying to convince her to go along with his plan and marry him.

The lawyers he and his brothers had hired a couple of years ago when they took over Club Tahoe had given Hunt the name of the best family lawyer in town. The woman was already preparing for a custody battle, should it come down to one with Noah's grandparents.

Hunt couldn't let Abby and Noah dangle on their own without his protection. The longer he waited, the more nervous Noah's grandparents made him. They'd already taken Noah from Abby once, and what was to stop them from trying again? So Hunt had wasted no time in planning the wedding. But now that it was here, the magnitude of his actions had his head spinning.

"I now pronounce you husband and wife," the attendant said, forcing Hunt's attention on the present.

He was *married*. To Abby.

Somehow, what he'd avoided for so long—marriage, a commitment—didn't feel painful at all. It felt almost right.

Huh.

He looked down at the beautiful woman at his side.

"Kiss the bride!" Noah said, and jumped up and down.

Hunt glanced past Abby to the back of the chapel. Despite the shit Levi had given him, he'd shown up with Emily, along with the rest of Hunt's brothers and a few of their friends, including Jaeger and Cali. Jaeger was one of Adam's best friends, and Hunt had known him since school. The chapel held enough witnesses to make the marriage real.

Because the marriage was real. *But not real.*

Abby was watching him, chewing the corner of her mouth and not exactly meeting his eyes.

This was a real wedding, even if he and Abby knew it was only temporary. And at real weddings, the groom kissed the bride. He'd been imagining how her lips would feel since the day they'd met. Who was he to pass up an opportunity?

Hunt leaned down and touched the underside of Abby's jaw. He pressed his mouth to hers.

Electric sparks set off everywhere their skin touched. Heat coursed through him, settling deep. He lingered, distracted as he sampled her mouth, forgetting everything but the feel of her lips against his, her soft skin...and heard Noah giggle.

Hunt lifted his head and locked his gaze with Abby's. Her eyes were half lidded, the pupils dilated.

Damn and shit. This was bad.

He was married, and he wanted his fake wife with every breath in his body.

CHAPTER SEVENTEEN

After the ceremony, the wedding party moved to Wes and Kaylee's place, where Wes had arranged a small reception. His brothers understood Hunt wanted to protect Abby and her son, but they didn't know the marriage was a farce, and Hunt wasn't about to tell them. Admitting he'd married a woman he didn't love would only prove Levi's point that Hunt was reckless, and it wouldn't look good if Noah's grandparents discovered the truth. This marriage needed to appear real.

Kaylee crossed the room, Harlow nowhere in sight. Not in this crowd, with all four uncles and their best friends within grabbing distance. It was a pass-the-baby event. Someone seriously needed to have another kid or Harlow would grow up to be the most spoiled child on the planet.

Kaylee grabbed Abby's hand and looked at Hunt. "I've already talked it over with Abby. Noah's going to stay with me and Wes this evening so you guys can have a proper wedding night."

Hunt looked at Abby, whose expression was a stiff, unnatural grin. *Great.*

"That's not necessary," he said.

"It's all arranged." Kaylee looked over her shoulder to where the kids were playing, Harlow crawling all over Noah, and Noah laughing loudly at the baby's aggressive antics. "The kids are getting along great, and we'd really love to do this for you."

Hunt raised an eyebrow at Abby. *Your call.*

Abby sighed and her shoulders loosened. Her forced smile turned genuine. "We'd love that. Thank you again for the offer. Noah is already close to you from Club Kids, so this is perfect."

Kaylee beamed. "So it's all set." She squeezed Abby's hand and walked off to where Wes stood with Bran and Ireland.

Hunt leaned down. "Are you sure?" he said out of the corner of his mouth, nodding a smile at Cali, Jaeger's wife, who was waggling her eyebrows pointedly at Abby and shooting him knowing looks.

"It's what's expected," Abby whispered. "We will be living together, won't we? Because I don't think I can explain to Noah's grandparents why I'm married, but not living with my husband."

Living together had crossed his mind, but in all the preparation this week, it had also been low on the priority list of things to discuss with Abby. "Of course we'll live together," he said confidently, then hesitated. "Where do you want to live?"

"I think it will be best if we live at my place. It's small, I know, but I don't want to disrupt Noah's life more than I already have with the marriage. Are you okay with that?"

Hunt thought about the layout of Abby's cottage. "It's a one bedroom?"

"Two, but Noah's room is more like a glorified closet."

"So we'd share a room," he said, and gauged her reaction.

Abby swallowed. "Y-yes. If that's okay. I can sleep on a cot and tuck it away when Noah is awake."

He'd prefer they *shared* a bed. He could keep his hands to himself.

Fine, that was a lie. No way could he keep his hands to himself. Not with Abby's soft, feminine scent and sexy body next to him. He'd try to seduce her into his arms. "I'll sleep on the floor. You'll take the bed." His tone was firm, but damn if he'd let his wife sleep on a cot.

An hour later, Abby was kissing Noah goodbye, and Hunt was standing with his brothers.

"Don't do anything I wouldn't," Wes said, and triple-winked.

"You have protection?" Bran asked. "Nothing like an unplanned honeymoon baby."

Typical coming from Bran, the most careful of Hunt's brothers.

"This isn't my first time at the rodeo," he told Bran. "I'm covered."

Not that he'd *need* anything covered. He wished he needed something covered, because his wife, yes, *wife*, looked incredible, and his body was desperate to be near her. What was taking her so long, anyway?

Just then, Adam walked up. "This is for you and Abby, courtesy of Blue Casino." He handed Hunt a bottle. "Feel free to bust it out tonight. You look a little nervous."

Hunt glanced at the Dom Perignon. Nervous? Damn straight he was nervous. He had to somehow keep his hands off his beautiful wife for an entire evening, without even the blessed distraction of Noah. Hunt choked out a laugh and thanked Adam.

Levi pointed at Hunt. "Remember what I told you."

Bran, Adam, and Wes all sighed.

"Levi," Wes said. "Give it a rest."

Levi bristled, but he shook out his shoulders and let out a breath. "Here." He shoved a small box at Hunt's chest. "It's from Emily." He coughed. "For your wedding night." Was that the sound of Levi's teeth grinding? "They're scented candles and some other frilly stuff Emily thought you guys might like."

Just hearing the words "scented candles" come out of Levi's mouth was gift enough.

"Thank you," he said, trying not to laugh at his gruff older brother. Emily might actually domesticate Levi, given enough time.

Champagne under one arm, scented candles in hand, Hunt made the rounds and said goodbye to his friends and family. On the outside, he was a man eager to get his bride alone. On the inside, he was a man eager to get his bride alone, but wasn't actually allowed to touch her.

Good times.

Hunt went to retrieve Abby, who was having a hard time saying goodbye, and Kaylee latched on to his arm, pulling him aside. "I don't know what all is going on with you and this whirlwind wedding, but try to make it work. I really like Abby, and I think she'll be good for you."

Hunt's face froze for half a second. Until he remembered no one knew what he and Abby had agreed to. "I married her, Kaylee. I'm going to take care of her." And that was the truth, even if the marriage was fake.

"It's not that. Abby has shit going on; we all know it at Club Kids. There's something off about the grandparents…" She shook her head. "I don't know what I'm saying. Just try to not mess it up, okay?"

Hunt's heart pounded and his chest tightened. Real or not, this marriage would need to stand—at least in the short term.

Hunt leaned down and kissed Kaylee on the cheek, which earned him a loud shout from Wes.

"Back off the brunette!" Wes said.

"I got this," Hunt said to Kaylee, and she smiled. But Hunt's chest didn't loosen. He was making promises he wasn't sure he could keep.

He walked up to Abby and Noah and ruffled the boy's hair. "Be good tonight, okay? If you need anything, have Kaylee call us."

"Bye, Mom. Bye, Hunt." Noah ran off to where he'd been playing with Adam and Harlow and a stack of foam blocks.

Abby looked up, amused. "It seems we're not needed."

He grabbed her hand. "Guess not. Ready to go?"

She nodded, and Hunt gestured for her to precede him.

Abby walked out the front doorway, and his gaze lingered on her perfectly molded ass and bared shoulders in the sundress. He was a man; he liked beautiful women. But he was inherently attracted to Abby, and that was the biggest problem of all.

Hunt huffed out a sigh and followed her out the door.

It was going to be a long night.

CHAPTER EIGHTEEN

As soon as Abby and Hunt returned to the house, she took off her heels and started putting away clothes and dishes she hadn't had time to put away before her harried rush to the chapel...

She was *married*.

Abby had been in love, she'd had a child, but she'd never been married. And now she was married to Hunt Cade, a man who didn't love her.

But he liked her. She felt it every time he looked at her. And she liked him too.

Abby studied Hunt as he pulled off his suit jacket, his strong arms and flat stomach defined through the fine linen of his shirt.

She cleared her throat and opened the fridge. "Are you hungry?"

Hunt snorted. "Are you? My brother provided food for a party of fifty instead of twenty. Hate to see good food go to waste, which means I might have overeaten." He patted his flat stomach. "Not sure I can fit anything more in here."

Abby closed the fridge and turned around. She wasn't hungry either, but what were they going to do all night?

She needed to keep busy or her mind would wander to the handsome man she now called husband. And that made her think of other things.

It had been years since she'd been with a man. Sad but true. Not like she had time for relationships. But she was in one now. Only she couldn't have sex with Hunt. That would complicate the situation to mass proportions. As long as things remained platonic, she and Hunt were good. At least, that was what she was telling herself. "Do you want to watch a movie?"

His eyes narrowed, and Abby got the feeling he read her mind.

He lifted a bottle off the coffee table she'd seen him carrying inside. "I have a better idea. Why don't we open the champagne Adam and Hayden gave us and toast to our future?"

Abby squeezed her hands together. Alcohol and sexual frustration were not a good combination, but maybe they could tackle another issue. "Sure, this will give us a chance to figure out how to make the marriage look real without little ears around." Between their two work schedules and her son, she and Hunt hadn't had time to lay out the specifics of their new reality after the wedding.

Hunt popped the cork and poured fizzing liquid into two mismatched champagne glasses Abby had found in the back of a cupboard. "The only way to make it look real is to act like it's real." He tipped his glass and clinked it to hers.

Abby sipped the tart liquid, her tongue tingling. "What do you mean, 'act like it's real'?"

Hunt sank into a chair at the two-person dining table. She'd have to buy a folding chair if they all wanted to eat together. "We act like a married couple. We live together, as planned, and are affectionate."

"Affectionate?" It had been so long that she was starved for affection, but... "Won't that confuse things?"

Hunt set his glass down. "Abby, if we have any hope of showing we're a united front and providing a solid household for Noah, we need to look like a married couple."

She bit her lip. "But...what does that look like?"

He laughed. "Damned if I know. Never had one myself. You?"

"My parents are still married, but they don't like each other."

He nodded thoughtfully. "So we're both in the dark. Well, we'll just have to make the best of it. Why don't we start by getting to know each other better?"

"Isn't that what we're doing?"

"Not yet, but we will," he said.

And why did that send prickles running down her arms?

"Have you ever heard of a game called 'Never Have I Ever'?" he asked.

"Don't they play that on *Ellen*?"

"The talk show? Maybe, but I think it originated on college campuses." His eyes twinkled and he sipped his champagne.

"I didn't finish college. And I was with Trevor while I was taking courses, so I didn't party much."

"See." He grinned. "I just learned something about you. And for the record, I never finished college either. I applied and got into a few places, but decided to run my boat-touring business instead. The money was too good to pass up." At her questioning glance, he rubbed his chin. "I stopped asking my father for money before I graduated high school. Was too stubborn to ask him to help with college."

Abby's mouth gaped. "Your family owns Club Tahoe, and you're filthy rich. Yet you turned down family money... to run a boating business?"

"Still want to be married to me?"

He was a complex man, her new husband. And devilishly handsome when he looked at her like that, with a crooked grin. "Yes." And not only because he could help her with Noah. Hunt was easy to be around. And kind. Honestly, the thought of marriage to him was a little too exciting for Abby's delicate heart.

Better not mention that or he might change *his* mind.

"Good," he said. "Because I'm not sure I'll let you go now that I have you."

He was killing her. How was she supposed to resist this man?

"To explain things a little more, me and my brothers hated Club Tahoe. Never wanted anything to do with the place."

Abby nearly choked on her next sip of champagne, which was surprisingly good, considering she wasn't much of a bubbly drink person when it didn't contain caffeine. "Hated it? But you own it. You work there."

"Maybe the word *hate* is too strong. The club was a symbol of our father's abandonment in favor of work. In favor of Club Tahoe. But we've made changes to the joint. Made it our own." He shook his head. "I don't know. I haven't thought about it since my father passed. My brothers and I just knew we couldn't let the place crumble after his death. Club Tahoe employs hundreds of people in the area. Didn't feel right ruining good employment for others... It's complicated." He frowned.

She didn't like the look on his face. Hunt wasn't a gloomy person, and she wanted to kiss that frown away. Which was a dangerous road for her mind to go down.

"Well, *my* past is simple," she said to lighten the mood, since kissing wasn't an option. "I grew up poor and lived in a small Midwestern town in the double-wide trailer my parents have rented for as long as I can remember. I moved to Tahoe on a whim after a friend said good money could be made working at the casinos. The closest university was over three hours away back home. In Tahoe I could work at a casino during the high season and take classes at the community college or in Reno, if I was careful with my money. But after my first year, I met Trevor. And got pregnant." She shrugged. "The rest is history."

Hunt's expression softened, but he still didn't look happy. "I'm sorry things were so hard for you, Abby."

She didn't want his pity. That wasn't why she'd told him about her past. She wanted to distract Hunt from the things that were making him sad. And she wanted for him to know where she came from, so there were no secrets.

"How does this 'Never Have I Ever' game work?" Abby said, changing the subject.

His eyes lit up. "Now we're talking. It's really very simple."

Hunt was easy to please. Where Trevor could be selfish and needy, Hunt was giving and supportive. He had depths he didn't often show, like when he spoke of his father and brothers, and he was making it extremely difficult to look at him as simply a handsome, rich guy.

"I say 'Never have I ever,' and follow it with something I haven't done," he said. "Like 'Never have I ever tightroped.' If you've tightroped before, you take a sip of your drink. If you haven't, you do nothing."

"So this is a drinking game?"

"Well, yeah. But maybe not with champagne." Hunt stood and scoured the fridge and cabinets, looking at home and incredibly large in her tiny kitchen. He pulled out orange juice and a five-year-old bottle of vodka. "I'll make them weak," he said, and winked.

"Wise, unless you want to get to know me hugging the toilet."

He laughed and handed her a new glass. "We'll go easy." He narrowed his eyes on her face. "Never have I ever...lived with a woman."

"Wow, way to kick the game off with a bang," she said, and grinned. Abby took a sip.

"It's 'lived with a man' in your case, not boy," he said.

Again, she took a sip. "I lived with Trevor."

He nodded. "You had a child together; it makes sense that you would have lived with him."

"But I'm the first woman you've lived with?" Seemed hard to believe no woman had nabbed Hunt before now.

"Yes," he said, and his brow furrowed. "Come to think of it, Noah is the first child I've lived with too."

"Wow, we're really throwing you into the deep end. Are you going to freak out at the sight of my tampons?"

Hunt choked on his drink. "Uh, no. I'm very familiar with the female body and all its complexities. Probably more familiar than you are." His eyes sparkled, the devil!

Abby's face heated. "I doubt that, and it's my turn. Never have I ever...been on a boat."

Hunt took a quick drink then set his glass down with a loud *thunk*. "*Never?*"

She shook her head.

"But how can that be? You've lived in Lake Tahoe for at least as long as Noah's been alive, so five, six years."

"I don't know. I didn't live anywhere near water growing up. Then I moved here and met Trevor soon after. We lived in a nice house and he took me to cool places, but I've never been on a boat. I always wanted to take a trip on the lake. Not sure why I didn't. I guess pregnancy and child-rearing put a damper on that dream."

He grunted. "Well, that's gonna change. You'll be on one of my boats before the week is out."

"I didn't say it to make you feel bad. It's just something I knew I could get you to drink on." She smiled mischievously.

His eyes widened. "You learn quickly, young Jedi."

She laughed, and the game went on. Abby shared the age she received her first kiss—twelve, and it was awful—and a few places where she'd never had sex. Hunt, of course, drank for every one of the places she'd mentioned, the naughty boy. And then he threw something out there few people knew about her.

"Never have I ever," Hunt said, "ridden a bull."

Abby drank.

He set his glass down, his gaze sharpening until she shrank back in her seat. "Oh, I gotta hear this story."

"Technically, it wasn't a real bull. It was a mechanical bull, and my friend made me do it."

"Famous last words, Mrs. Cade."

Abby blinked. "I forgot my name will change."

"Only if you want it to. Now finish the bull-riding story."

She cleared her throat, clinging to the game and not the notion of her married name. "On the drive to California, I stopped off at a friend's house in Texas. She had a favorite bar, and there was a bull-riding thingy."

He laughed. "Did you fall off right away?"

She sent him a scathing look. "No, I did not, *Mr. Cade*. I rode that bull and I rode him hard and long."

Hunt gulped, took a swig of his drink, then shifted in his seat. "So, you what? Won the bull-riding contest?"

"Would you like to see my medal?"

His eyes rounded. "You're shitting me."

"Nope."

"Damn." He sat back and absently rubbed his mouth. "Call me impressed."

Abby yawned, despite the sexy image Hunt was presenting. When he touched his mouth, she thought of his lips touching hers like they had in the chapel. And he hadn't made the kiss quick. It had lingered and stirred things down low that had lain dormant for years. But it was past two in the morning and she was exhausted after her wedding day. And now it was her wedding night...

"Tired?" Hunt asked.

"A little, you?"

"I could sleep. You mind if I take a quick shower?"

"Help yourself. Towels are in the hall closet." Abby returned to the sink, where she pushed around dishes, distracted. *Hunt, naked, in the shower...*

Keep your head clear!

While Hunt used the bathroom, Abby quickly put away the dishes and changed into sleep shorts and a T-shirt. She stared at the bed that seemed to engulf her small room.

"I'll take the floor," Hunt said, surprising her from behind and making her jump.

"Oh," she said, and spun around. "There's no need for you to sleep on the floor. I have the cot."

"Nah," he said, and grabbed a blanket from a small chair in the corner. He lifted it. "You mind?"

"No, but are you sure you'll be comfortable?" She

worried her lip as he laid the blanket in a makeshift pallet on the floor.

"Perfectly," he said, lying down and tucking his arm behind his head, his biceps bulging.

Abby quickly looked away. This was too intimate. *Too intimate!*

She hurried to the closet, grabbed an extra pillow, and pulled a fresh pillowcase over it.

She handed the pillow to Hunt and frowned. "I don't feel right having you sleep on the floor. What about the couch?"

Hunt shook his head. "We need to get used to sleeping in the same bedroom. Without Noah around, this is the perfect opportunity to get comfortable with the idea."

Abby got the feeling that Hunt was too comfortable with the idea of sleeping in her bedroom, and all of this was for her sake. "That makes sense."

She slid back the blankets and climbed into bed, trying not to look at the handsome man on the floor. "Good night."

A manly yawn rose from the side of the bed. "Night, wife."

CHAPTER NINETEEN

Abby woke in a cocoon of warmth. She smiled, wiggled her toes, and then froze. Her eyes flew open. Hunt was in bed with her.

She vaguely remembered him returning from the bathroom and half consciously sliding into bed with her last night. He'd been out of it, and she couldn't bring herself to send him to the blanket on the floor.

In the middle of the night, it hadn't seemed like a big deal. Only it was morning now, and instead of sleeping on his side, his back to her, one large leg was now tucked between hers and his arm was around her waist, his face snuggled between her breasts.

Oh God. Why did he have to be a cuddler on top of everything else?

Abby looked down at his light brown hair cut close, the top slightly longer and ruffled from sleep. The scent of her shower soap and his clean skin wafted to her nose, and she breathed it in. Hunt smelled really good. And he was super cuddly, even if his cheek was smashed on top of her breast.

She glanced up and considered her options. Slide out

from under him and try to not wake him? He'd still realize he'd gotten into bed with her—a reasonable mistake in the middle of the night—but better if he didn't know the compromising position their bodies had inadvertently sought.

Before Abby could figure out the most strategic escape route, Hunt breathed in, his head rubbing her breast, mouth fluttering over her nipple.

A sharp spear of arousal hit Abby square between her legs where his warm thigh rested, putting pressure to the heat. She sucked in a breath, her body freezing in place. She needed to wake him.

Only his hand began roaming down her leg now, and *his* leg slid up, rubbing the spot where she pulsed with need.

Her mind spun. On the one hand, her body craved him. It had been so long, and Hunt was incredible, inside and out. But...

What were the buts?

They *were* married. And they needed to make this relationship look real. Sex would definitely bring them closer.

Oh right, *but*... What happened when Hunt left her and Noah to continue on with his life?

Abby knew herself. She liked Hunt. She'd always liked him. Well, after she realized he wasn't simply some hot guy trying to pick her up at a club for a casual fling. He was a genuine guy who cared for her son. So much so that he was willing to marry her to keep Noah safe. And the way Hunt looked at her made her tingle, wishing to be closer. Of course she'd fall in love with him if she let things progress. Which was why she couldn't allow that to happen.

Hunt moaned and pulled down her T-shirt, peppering the space between her breasts with soft kisses, his long fingers brushing over her nipples.

"Oh," she said, a breath escaping her mouth.

Hunt froze. He lifted his head and stared at her with half-lidded, groggy eyes. He glanced down at her body, and his hands on her body, and pulled back as though he'd been burned.

"Morning," she said.

"Morning," he said hesitantly. He looked around the room toward his pallet on the floor. "I have no idea how I ended up here. I'm really sorry." He stared at his hand. "And sorry for this..."

She grinned, trying to make light of an awkward situation. "Don't be. It was the most action I've gotten in years."

Hunt's eyes narrowed. For the longest moment, he didn't say anything. And then his leg shifted ever so slightly between her thighs.

She sucked in a breath. "Hunt."

His eyes darkened and sparks ping-ponged between them. Why did the man have to be so sexy?

"You know," he said idly, touching the edge of her lip with a lightly callused finger, "we could consummate this marriage. Make it official."

Her chest fluttered, despite all the reasons it should stop acting stupid and keep itself cool. "That would complicate things." No way was she mentioning her real fear. The one where she fell for the handsome player who was merely doing her a favor and helping her out of a tough situation.

"It's really the right thing to do, if you consider it," he said. "If the grandparents ever suspect our marriage is fake, they can't say it isn't legitimate, and you and Noah will be safe."

"True," she said. "But then we'd have to deal with the aftermath of having sex."

He raised an eyebrow. "There's an aftermath?"

"Yes. We might want to do it again. And we're not in a real relationship."

"Hmm..." His gaze was on her chest and moving lower. "I'm willing to take a chance if you are."

She didn't respond, because her brain had locked in a hormone haze.

He leaned down and touched his lips to hers, softer than he had at the chapel. He cupped the side of her head, giving her ample time to pull away.

That infernal leg nudged between hers ever so slightly, and he kissed her again. This time, it was a real kiss, with genuine passion behind it, sending her into a lust spiral.

Abby wrapped her arms around Hunt's broad shoulders and kissed him back.

He didn't rush things and take advantage, but his hand wandered slowly, leaving a wake of fire in its path.

Hunt dragged his lips down her neck, his fingers grazing over her nipple until she thought she would lose her mind. Finally, he palmed her breast, and her body arched.

He slid her T-shirt up. "Okay?"

They were *getting to know* each other. That was good, right?

Abby raised her arms, and off went her T-shirt, leaving her breasts bared.

Hunt took in a deep breath and touched the underside of one breast, kissing the top at the same time. "You're a beautiful woman, Abby. Have I mentioned that?"

His large leg was still between hers, and her eyes were going crossed with the double stimulation of his mouth and hand on her breast, and his leg nudging ever so often the apex of her sex. "Uh, I don't think so."

Could a woman climax from a minute of touching? Because she was beginning to feel flutters of an orgasm, and she'd swear she was close. This was what happened when you didn't have sex for an ice age. "Maybe we should stop."

"Do you want to stop?"

"I don't want to have sex." Even if her body was calling out to him, a part of her brain was clear enough to know some boundaries. Not many, clearly, but some.

He lifted his head. "No sex, then. How about I pleasure you?"

Her eyes widened. "Um," she said, and he smiled.

"When you think about it, it's my job. You know, as your husband."

Her jaw dropped.

"What?" he said, a lock of soft brown hair brushing his forehead. "This is the least I can do for my new wife."

"You're crazy, Hunt Cade."

"You married me, Abby Cade."

Did that have to sound so sexy and possessive?

She reached up and kissed him. Hard.

Hunt shifted, removing his leg, and she nearly whimpered in regret. "Just getting into a better position," he said, and touched the inside of her thigh with his warm palm.

There went the flutters, her abdomen contracting. This wouldn't take long. And was having an orgasm with your husband really such a bad thing? "More," she murmured.

Hunt kissed her, gripping her hip, his massive erection against her leg indicating his arousal. And then his mouth trailed over the swell of her breast.

He tongued her nipple and slid his hand beneath her shorts, caressing up and down the crease between her thigh and her sex, not quite touching any of the good parts.

He was killing her.

Abby ran a hand down Hunt's bared chest, momentarily got distracted by the ridges of his abs, and made her way to the waistband of his boxer briefs.

He froze, staying her palm. "We can't do that or I might lose it. And I *really* don't want to lose it until you do, wife."

There he went again, with the sexy fake-husband talk.

He slipped his finger between her legs, found her sex, and swirled light circles in the spot that had been shooting off sparks since she woke in his arms.

She saw stars, but thought she could hold off orgasming and embarrassing herself after only a few strokes.

Then his mouth came over her nipple and he sucked.

She lost it. Screamed. Flailed on the bed—just totally lost it.

And man, was it good.

When Abby came down to earth from the best orgasm she could remember, Hunt was kissing her chest, finding her hand and twining their fingers together. "I think I'm going to enjoy my husbandly duties. Care for another?"

She blinked, realized how far she'd allowed things to go, and couldn't find it within herself to care. Still... "I don't know if this was such a good idea."

"Regrets?"

She shook her head slowly. "I should regret it, but I really, really don't."

He sent her a crooked grin, and her gaze dropped to his mouth.

Hunt was trouble.

CHAPTER TWENTY

Abby was right. Hunt was fully committed to marriage for the sake of helping out her and Noah, but sex between them would change things. Not that it had ever changed things for him in the past, but technically, Abby was his wife. And he was really fucking attracted to her.

He hadn't been lying. He could give her orgasm after orgasm, and die a happy man. But she was smart to keep some distance between them. He couldn't imagine himself committed to one woman for the rest of his life, and not because he needed variety, like he told his brothers. He didn't have luck loving women, and he'd learned that the hard way.

Hunt was helping out a woman and child in need, that was all. And, fortunately for him, she was incredibly beautiful, especially when her lips parted and she cried out her release. He might explode of sexual frustration if this was what he had to look forward to every morning, but what an incredible way to go.

Now that he knew the way she tasted and the sexy sounds she made, he wanted to pleasure Abby and sink into her body. And he didn't imagine he'd be over it after one night, like his normal pattern. He could see himself wanting her again. Maybe a lot—like, say, every day—and then where would they be? In a relationship neither of them had chosen for the right reasons.

But this? Giving pleasure to a beautiful woman? Nope, not complicated. This was what Hunt had been born for, and there was no woman he wanted to please more than Abby.

Abby showered, and Hunt pulled his dress undershirt over his head, yanking up his suit pants. Not the most comfortable morning attire, but all he had at the moment. Which needed to change. It was time he officially moved in with Abby and Noah.

Abby exited the bathroom, rubbing her damp hair with a towel, her face flushed. "Are you hungry?"

"Yeah, but I've got that covered." Hunt walked into the kitchen to the fridge, reaching for a dish. He grabbed two plates and set out slices of chocolate cake with white buttercream. "Kaylee sent us home with a care package."

Abby stared at the food. "You want to eat our wedding cake for breakfast?"

"Is there a better time?"

She laughed and grabbed forks. "No, I guess not."

Abby sat across from Hunt and studied him. "Do you regret this morning? You're stuck with me for the time being. From what I hear, you players regret taking things *there*, if you can't make a smooth escape."

He snorted. "First of all, there's nothing in life better than waking to a beautiful, sexy woman whose company you enjoy. Second, have you any idea who you're talking to? What we did this morning, I could do all day and never grow tired." He pointed his fork at her. "Keep that in mind. I aim to please."

She sent him a look. "You're not here to please; you're here to help me with Noah's grandparents."

"You see, that's where we differ. You see this as a single-purpose situation, and I see it as dual-purpose, even if we just realized the second, far more pleasing benefit of our arrangement this morning." He winked. "I help you with the grandparents from hell, and we both enjoy the pleasure of each other's company." He shoved a huge bite of cake in his mouth and grinned.

Her eyes held a spark of humor. "And the player has returned."

Hunt held back a frown. Abby thought what everyone did. That he wasn't capable of a serious relationship. It was true, yet it bothered him. "Busted." Hunt polished off his cake and stood.

Abby looked up. "Where are you going?"

"As much as I like this suit, I need more clothes here if we're going to live together. I'm heading to my place to grab a few things." For a moment, Abby's light expression fell, and Hunt worried he'd said something wrong. "Or I can go later..."

"No." She waved him off. "Go. I have house stuff to do before Noah returns. I'll need to clear out a drawer or two for my *new husband*." She smiled, but her eyes didn't hold their normal spark.

Hunt hesitated, then leaned over and kissed Abby on the mouth. "I'll be back."

He'd show her there was nothing to worry about. He could keep things in check and still show Abby a good time. He had to, because he refused to let Abby and Noah down.

———

HUNT WENT to the place he rented on the lake, complete with a boat slip for his new Cobalt. The townhome was triple the size of Abby and Noah's house, yet he liked Abby's place better. It was filled with Noah's laughter, crispy bacon, and flowerpots that bloomed from Abby's touch.

Hunt scanned his home. Nope, not a damn thing lived in this place. It was where he showered and slept, and that was all.

He quickly packed up his clothes and toiletries and closed down the house. He'd already given his notice to the landlord, so there wasn't much left to do. The place had come furnished, and he'd already moved his Cobalt to the club dock.

Hunt had sent out a text to his brothers this morning while Abby showered, asking to meet up. It was his honeymoon week; the least his brothers could do was meet him for an hour.

His honeymoon... Okay, so he hadn't thought that part through. Was that what made Abby unhappy when he'd said he was taking off?

When Adam and Wes married their wives, Hunt and his brothers didn't see them for weeks, due to all the honeymooning (*sex*) they were engaged in. They had gone off the grid, and here Hunt was, the day after his wedding, and already he'd left his bride behind. But she wasn't in this for romance, though this morning's activities were promising on other fronts...

He scrubbed his fingers through his damp hair after the shower he'd taken at his old place. Somehow, he felt like he was already screwing things up. The meeting with his brothers was for her. Maybe she'd understand once he explained.

Hunt pulled up to Levi's house, all of his brothers' cars parked in the front. He took a deep breath and stepped out of his Range Rover. *Now or never.*

He walked up the steps to the front porch and gave a courtesy rap on the door before stepping inside. "Greetings."

Hunt leaned down to pet Levi's dog Grace, who'd run up to him and proceeded to lick the crap out of his shoe and pant leg.

Wes yawned on the couch, and Levi had an arm around Emily's waist near the kitchen island.

Hunt did a double take. *Huh.* He'd never seen Emily in sweats and a T-shirt. She always wore work clothes, dressed in a skirt and blouse most days.

Adam poured himself a mug of coffee, his hair sticking up at odd angles. Jesus, you'd think it was the crack of dawn. "Look'n good, everyone," Hunt said.

Bran kicked up his socked feet and leaned back on the recliner. "We all have plans. What's this emergency about?"

Hunt scanned their casual clothes and wrinkled T-shirts. Didn't look like they had plans. "You don't look busy."

"Some of us like to spend time with our women on the weekend," Levi said. "What's your problem, leaving your wife the day after your wedding? Didn't think you'd be looking for an escape this soon."

There it was, the judgment. Levi assumed Hunt didn't take the marriage seriously. He might not be doing it for the normal reasons, but he couldn't be more serious about caring for Abby and Noah.

Hunt pushed down the anger Levi's words filled him

with and focused on why he'd come. "Have any of you thought about the house and what we're going to do with it?"

As far as Hunt knew, none of them had set foot inside their family home since their father's death two years ago. The only person who entered the premises these days was Esther, their father's old receptionist.

Esther had always maintained their father's Tahoe mansion while he was alive. Made sense to have her check in on the place every once in a while, in between her "silver dating" life and senior boot camp classes.

"Haven't thought much about the old place," Levi said. "Been too busy keeping the resort going. Besides, Esther has things in hand."

"She says it's in good shape," Emily said. "But Esther also told me that it's pretty outdated. I've never personally seen the place." Emily shot Levi a glare, and Levi's eyes widened like a deer caught in the headlights.

"What?" Levi said. "That place is haunted, Emily. None of us want to go there."

"Yeeeah," Hunt said. "About that. What do you think about fixing it up? Maybe get the old house ready to sell?"

Adam stretched his arms above his head. "I suppose we should sell it. None of us want to live there."

"Well," Hunt said. "Maybe one person."

Adam's eyes narrowed. "What do you mean?"

Hunt needed a respectable place for him and Abby to live with Noah. The lawyer hadn't said as much, but it made sense for them to live in a home where no one could doubt their financial stability. Abby hadn't wanted to make any major changes in Noah's life after the wedding, but there would be weeks before the Cade estate was ready to live in. If there was any house in Lake Tahoe that impressed, it was the Cade mansion, and Hunt wanted to put his best foot forward in case CPS came sniffing around like they had a few weeks ago.

No one hated their family home more than Hunt. The inside was cold as hell. Fortunately, the outside had been Hunt and his brothers' domain and haven. Their father never cared what they did outside, as long as the inside was pristine for the work associates he entertained.

"If you're interested in fixing the place up and selling it," Hunt said, "I could do the remodel. But I'd like to live there with Abby and Noah." No need to mention why he wanted the house for him and his new wife. His brothers were suspicious enough. If they knew his marriage was a farce to make it look like Abby was providing a solid foundation for her son, his brothers would never trust him again.

Trust was a fragile thing. Once you lost it, it was difficult to build back. Hunt had learned that the hard way.

"I suppose it's not the worst idea," Levi said. "As long as Abby doesn't mind. Could be messy remodeling."

Hunt leaned his shoulder against the wall. "I've considered that. I'd have Lewis do the demo and rough-in first."

Levi frowned. "You've already spoken to Lewis? And he agreed?"

"Well, not exactly." Construction during Tahoe summers was busy as hell. Which was why Hunt had broached the idea of the remodel with their friend Lewis, who owned Sallee Construction, *before* he brought it up to his brothers. "He's busy, but one of the projects they were about to work on is being held up in the permit department. He has a waitlist, but he's willing to put us at the top, if we can start now."

"No point in holding on to the place if we're not going

to use it," Bran said, shrugging. "The resort is stable and running efficiently. It's not a bad idea to tackle this now."

Levi scowled. "I don't know."

Hunt internally groaned. Of course Levi would doubt him.

"I'm game for Hunt to spearhead it," Bran said, and looked at Wes.

"Game," Wes agreed from the couch.

Adam checked his watch. "As long as I don't have to do it, I'm open. Maybe we should hire a decorator for the upgrades, though. I'm not sure I trust Hunt's taste."

"First of all," Hunt said, "I have excellent taste. However, Lewis already put me in touch with a decorator, because I can admit when I'm in over my head."

"Not always," Levi mumbled.

Hunt stretched his neck, the tendons popping with the motion. Cool, he needed to remain cool. Leaping across the room to tackle his brother because he was being an ass wouldn't convince the rest of them that he could do this. But before Hunt could explode all over Levi, Adam saved him.

"Then it's settled," Adam said, and walked to the front door. "Gotta go, but keep me posted."

Hunt looked at Levi, who hadn't agreed. Emily nudged him in the ribs. "Fine," he said.

Good enough for Hunt. Not like he'd do much better when it came to Levi.

With a spring in his step, Hunt took off to tell Abby the good news. Or what he hoped would be good news. She hadn't wanted big changes for Noah, but this was *all* for Noah. She'd agree.

Obviously, he didn't know women well. At least, not this woman.

CHAPTER TWENTY-ONE

"A new house?" Abby said. She set down the laundry basket she'd been carrying. "I told you, I don't want to disrupt Noah's life any more than I already have." Hunt hadn't listened to her. He was ignoring her wishes and making decisions behind her back. Her pulse throbbed, heart hammering a mile a minute. What had she done marrying him?

Hunt raised his hands. "Hear me out. Technically, it's not a new house; it's the home I grew up in. And we wouldn't move for weeks. There's demo and rough-in construction that needs to take place. I don't want my family living through that."

His family. But she and Noah weren't his. Unless Hunt was taking this marriage more seriously than she'd initially thought. But why would he do that?

"Just consider it, okay?" he said. "We could take Noah by and see what needs to be done."

"So it's not a done deal. You haven't made a major decision behind my back."

Hunt placed his hand over his heart. "I'd never do something so stupid."

Abby glanced around. Her place wasn't much, but it was cozy. Okay, a little *too* cozy. "Why now?"

"My brothers and I have put off dealing with our family estate for years. That's one reason. The other is I think living in the house where I grew up will help put off Vivian. I'm not one for fancy shit, but my father was, and the house he built is impressive. We'd live in luxury, close to the resort and your job, and best of all, there'd be no rent. The place is paid off. You can save money."

Now he was speaking her language. No rent? She'd love to save some of her earnings instead of throwing it out the door on Tahoe's housing expenses. "Not that I'm agreeing to anything, but are your brothers okay with this?"

Hunt snorted. "My brothers are happy to hand off the work of remodeling the old joint. We're paying for the upkeep anyway while it's vacant. Might as well move forward on a remodel and prepare it for sale."

Abby had never been given anything for free in her life. Until Hunt came along. And she wasn't sure how she felt about it. Yes, it was wonderful to have someone do kind things for her, but what could she possibly give him to compensate for all he'd done? "Are you sure your brothers won't feel like we're taking advantage?"

"Hell no. We're doing them a favor."

Abby let out a breath and walked into the kitchen, resting her hands on the worn Formica countertop. "I'll agree to take Noah by, but if he seems uncomfortable for any reason or doesn't want to leave our home, I won't agree to this arrangement."

"Fair enough."

———

"WHEEE!" Noah shouted as he ran around the front yard of the Cade estate, and Abby flinched. Clearly she'd misjudged her son's enthusiasm for a new home. Especially one that was a three-story, modern mountain mansion.

Hunt quirked his eyebrow at her.

"Fine," she said. "So he likes the yard." She looked up at the front door. "But this place is massive. What if he gets lost?"

Hunt nodded sagely, though she knew she was being ridiculous. "Always a consideration. However, my brothers and I never did, and I'm confident in Noah. He'll probably know the place better than either of us in a day or two. But let's not jump to conclusions." Was that a confident smile on Hunt's face? "Let's take a look inside and see what Noah thinks."

Yes, that most definitely was confidence oozing off Hunt. Dammit. He knew something Abby didn't.

He jogged up the steps to the front door and punched a code into a keypad.

The door opened and Abby's breath caught. "Holy shit."

"*Mom*," Noah said, giggling.

"I mean, holy cow." She was already setting a bad example, her roots of growing up in a double-wide showing through.

"Wow!" Noah said, looking around in amazement. "Do you really live here?"

Hunt crouched next to Noah and scanned the room, with two-story ceilings and windows that looked out onto the woods. "When I was a kid I did. What do you think?"

"It's huge," Noah said, eyes bright. "Can I run around?"

"Have at it."

Noah took off like a shot, past the foyer and down a long hall. Abby could hear him whooping and hollering the entire way.

She sent Hunt a sidelong glance. "This doesn't mean anything."

He smiled. "Whatever you say, wife."

A shiver ran down her spine. His words were meant in humor, but somehow she thought he enjoyed calling her wife, and that was the part that messed with her head. "Are you sure you've never been married before? Because you seem to have all the appropriate responses to get what you want."

He chuckled. "Never been married. But I'm attentive."

"Which is why you're so good with women," she said, not liking her own words.

Hunt grabbed her hand, his smile fading. "We had a deal, Abby. I'm committed to you while we're together."

Prickles raced down her arm where his warm palm held hers. She was reading into things. Wondering if there could be more.

She slowly slid her hand out of his and walked through the dining room and into the kitchen. Hunt's footsteps sounded behind her.

She glanced over her shoulder and caught him staring off, a serious expression on his face as he looked around the kitchen.

She forgot her worries about their marriage. What did this house really mean to Hunt?

He wanted her to live here, but as soon as he'd stepped inside, his demeanor turned guarded. "Everything okay?"

He nodded. "Just haven't been back here in a while."

His shoulders shook ever so slightly. "It's older than I remember. This kitchen is crap."

The "kitchen" was top-of-the-line fancy, and a million times better than the one she shared with Noah. Hunt never seemed to mind her place, but the mountain mansion he hated? If they moved into Hunt's family home, it would be the finest thing Abby had ever lived in.

However, she could see how if they planned to sell the estate, they'd need to remodel the kitchen. It had to be twenty years old. Anyone spending that kind of money would expect something modern. Still, he was awfully tetchy over an outdated kitchen. "Is that all that's wrong?"

Hunt shoved his hands in his jean pockets and stood there stiffly, not answering. Or unable to.

There was something about this house that set him off. If they were going to live here, she wanted to make sure *he* was going to be happy with the decision. She tried another tactic. "What was it like growing up here?"

"Cold," he said, no inflection in his tone.

Abby laughed darkly. "And you want us to move in?"

Hunt looked around, letting out a long sigh. "It's temporary. Besides, I plan to strip the place until it's practically unrecognizable."

Her eyebrows pinched together. "What's the real reason you don't like this house?"

He glanced to the side, seemingly looking for Noah. Abby could hear her son racing across the upstairs level. "My childhood was...different. It wasn't awful, but it was lonely. My mother died when I was a baby, and my father was a workaholic. When he was around, he wasn't attentive. I don't know." His shoulders jerked up in a stiff shrug. "There were five of us, and we were a handful. Can't say I blame him for wanting to ditch us."

Abby swallowed, pain shooting through her chest. She wanted to hug Hunt. She wanted to yell at his father and tell him he should have been there for his sons. Here she was fighting to raise her son, and Hunt's father had thrown his chance to parent his children away.

Abby settled for looping her arm through Hunt's, unsure how a man—*her husband*—would feel about it. "You're the best with the children at Club Tahoe, and Noah loves you. If you didn't have a happy childhood, it doesn't show."

He looked away. "I don't like to see the kids lonely. Besides," he said, and grinned. "According to my brothers, I'm the same age as them mentally. We're a good fit."

Abby squeezed his arm. "Your brothers are wrong. You're a wonderful man, and you'll make a great father. You're already a wonderful role model to Noah."

Hunt studied her, as though to gauge her seriousness. And then heat filled his eyes, and his gaze swept her face, landing on her mouth.

Abby's mind shot back to yesterday morning and the look on Hunt's face when he was giving her incredible pleasure.

Good Lord, he was potent.

She cleared her throat. "We should find Noah. I think he's lost in the labyrinth." She made to pull away, and Hunt placed his hand on top of hers.

"Abby." He waited until she met his eyes. "I won't let you down."

He'd read her mind, because she *was* afraid. Though not of him. She was afraid she felt too much for someone she couldn't have.

CHAPTER TWENTY-TWO

Hunt couldn't get his balled hands to loosen as he walked through the old house, searching for Noah. What had he been thinking convincing Abby to move in?

When he'd made the decision, it was purely to protect Abby and Noah. He'd forgotten about the doom this place filled him with. And it all came crashing back, one memory after another with every room entered and every untouchable piece of furniture his eyes landed on.

Hunt found Noah in his old bedroom, and it took him back for a moment.

"This is your room," Noah said, lying on the carpet, arms folded behind his head instead of lying on top of the extra-long twin bed shoved against the wall. "When we live here, I want your room."

Unlike the rest of the house, Hunt's old bedroom didn't upset him. It had been his refuge. "How do you know this was my room?"

Noah jumped up and ran to the walk-in closet. He pointed at the inside doorjamb.

Hunt was here was carved into the wood.

He'd carved that when he was eight years old, only a few years older than Noah.

Hunt's father hadn't come home one night, and Hunt and his brothers had been left with the housekeeper, who made them all go to bed at seven so she wouldn't have to deal with them. Hunt had sat in his closet and created a fort, staying up well past his bedtime. That was one of many nights he'd envisioned himself a pirate, a rescuer of the innocent.

Hunt shook his head. Someone should have taught his younger self the definition of a pirate. Even now, he instinctively considered any boat-ferrying man or woman a protector of the sea—or in Hunt's case, the lake. He'd promised himself, he'd rescue people, because no one ever rescued him. Yet the only thing keeping him brave right now and not running for the hills was Abby and Noah. This was for them.

Which was a scary thought.

Hunt was growing more and more attached to his new little family. He might be capable of helping them now, but he was no fool. Deep down, he knew his brothers were right. He'd screw up eventually, and he'd never be good to anyone in the long term.

Noah ran from bedroom to bedroom, oohing and aahing, and even Abby, his skeptical new bride, was beaming. The only people haunted by this place were Hunt and his brothers.

He'd strip the house bare, down to the studs if need be. One way or another, he'd make it a place he and Abby and Noah could enjoy.

Hunt ran a palm across his damp brow.

"Hunt," Abby said, standing behind him. He hadn't

heard her walk up, too caught up in the past. "We don't have to live here."

He was showing weakness over a damned house. That wouldn't do. "Does this mean you're considering it?"

She gestured across the hall to Noah, who was jumping on Wes's old bed. "I don't think I have a choice. Noah loves this place. But we don't have the history here that you do. We'll be just as happy at my house."

Hunt's back stiffened. The only redeeming qualities about Abby's house were the people who lived in it. Otherwise, the small cabin was run-down and in a shady location. It wasn't good enough for Noah and Abby. Not if they wanted to shut down Noah's grandparents from ever thinking they could gain custody of their grandchild.

Hunt needed to man up and shake off the past. "Then it's a done deal. We'll move in as soon as the rough-in is complete. You okay with Lewis's workers coming around? I know most of them, and I trust Lewis with my life."

"I trust you, so that works for me," she answered.

Hunt's chest tightened. No one ever gave him absolute trust. Women, his brothers—they all loved him, but they were smart enough to not trust him. Until Abby.

Only Abby was sweet and a loving, protective mom. She was no pushover. Yet she seemed to have absolute faith in him. How the hell had he managed that?

Damn this house. It was causing him to doubt himself, reminding him of the past and where he'd come from.

It was a means to an end, he told himself. The house impressed everyone, and it would put off Noah's grandparents. And he'd prove to his brothers he could take on the challenge of fixing it up.

Every one of his brothers had stepped up when it came

to Club Tahoe since they took over management, except Hunt. This was his way of showing his worth.

———

IT WAS late by the time Hunt drove Abby back to her place. She made a quick dinner of meatballs and pasta, and Hunt read Noah a book.

"One more!" Noah chanted from his bedroom, ecstatic his best friend from Club Tahoe was living with them now. Noah couldn't stop talking about their "new house," either.

Abby walked to the bedroom door. "No way, little guy. It's been a busy few days. You need your sleep."

Both Hunt and Noah frowned from the bed. Saddest sight she'd ever seen.

"Fine," she said. "One more, but then you have to go to sleep."

Noah jumped up and ran to the small bookcase, while Hunt looked on, smiling. The guy seemed as happy to read Noah another story as Noah was to hear it. Amazing.

After the last book, Abby and Hunt said good night to Noah, and Abby silently closed the door to his bedroom.

She shifted her feet in the hallway. "So..." she said.

"So," he replied, with a slight upward quirk to his lips.

Geez, this was awkward. They weren't a couple, yet they'd done some serious adulting in the bedroom the other morning.

Last night, they'd spent so much time unpacking and finding space for Hunt's things, with Noah coming in every two seconds, that their morning activities hadn't come up. Hunt had slept in the bed with Abby, but they'd both passed out as soon as the lights were off.

Tonight they were no longer exhausted from unpacking.

Would he expect what had happened yesterday to happen again? Did she want him to?

A wave of heat swept through her belly. Darn Hunt Cade and his hands. She could get used to them, and then where would she be? Alone and Hunt-less. "Do you want to use the bathroom first, or should I?"

"You go ahead," he said. "I have an email to shoot off to Lewis. I'd like to meet him at the house tomorrow and get his crew started on the demo."

Right, the demo. It was only Abby who was thinking about sexy time with Hunt. It was his fault; he was very good at it.

Get it together, woman!

Hunt had misgivings when it came to his family home. But maybe this was where she could repay him for all he was doing for her. She'd help him with the remodel, now that she didn't have to work extra shifts to make ends meet, and together they'd wipe away bad memories.

Abby brushed her teeth, changed into a nightshirt and shorts, and crawled into bed. She heard Hunt enter the bathroom, but by that time her eyelids were drooping and she could barely keep her eyes on the page of her book.

She set her novel on the nightstand. She was going to spend the night in bed with Hunt again, and a pleasure shiver racked her body. From here on out, they'd sleep in the same bed, now that Noah was around. Regardless of those scintillating thoughts, her exhaustion won the battle and she fell asleep.

What seemed like moments later, Abby opened her eyes to a bluish-gray light streaming in through the blinds. It was morning, but it had to be early.

She thought back to the night before. She must have passed out hard. She didn't remember Hunt coming into the bedroom, and now that she extended her senses, he wasn't in bed with her either. She distinctly remembered the size of Hunt's warm body next to her. There was no warmth, no swell of the mattress, no large arm possessively holding her.

Abby sat up. Had he already gone for the day? He'd seemed eager to meet with his friend Lewis to get the house repairs started...

And then Abby saw him.

Hunt was lying on the floor on a blanket, his naked torso on display. One arm curled under his head, hair ruffled, long lashes falling against strong cheekbones.

Abby drank in the sight like a starved woman. Her gaze trailed down from the bulging of his biceps, across wide, muscular shoulders, to a stomach with defined abs she couldn't look away from.

The other night, she'd not gotten a good enough look at the beauty that was Hunt Cade, because *sweet Jesus*.

When she glanced up, his eyes were open and on her. Staring at her staring at him. He'd caught her ogling, and he didn't seem to mind. Not one bit. In fact, he was looking at her like he wanted to take a bite of something.

This was bad.

"Mom?" Noah called groggily from the hallway.

"Crap." Abby glanced around. She was caught. Not for the sexy thoughts swimming through her head, but because Hunt was supposed to be in bed with her. Even Noah knew married people slept in the same bed. He'd informed her last night, when he worried she wouldn't know how to treat her new husband.

Hunt's eyes widened and he threw off the light blanket and jumped into bed with her. She'd only had a split second to take in his muscled legs before he was curling up against her body. His large erection pressed to her backside.

Abby squeaked, and Hunt squeezed her hip.

"*Shh,*" he said, and sent her a warning look.

How was she supposed to keep quiet with his large, aroused body pressed to hers?

"Your fault," he mumbled. "Can't look at me like that in the morning and not expect things to rise to the occasion."

She attempted to turn her head and say something saucy, but Noah walked in the room.

"Hi, sweetheart," Abby said, her voice higher than usual.

Noah climbed into bed, unaware of Abby's turmoil.

Hunt pulled her back even tighter against his body, making room for Noah.

"I slept good," Noah told them. Her son yawned. "What's for breakfast?"

Abby cleared her throat, and wrangled her mind off the hot, ridiculously sexy man holding her, and said, "Why don't you brush your teeth, and I'll make you some eggs?"

"French toast."

Abby brushed the light brown hair off Noah's brow and kissed his forehead. "French toast it is."

"Two slices, please," Noah said.

"I'll take six," Hunt said, and Noah giggled.

Abby's mouth twisted. "Considering you two are going to do most of the eating, I'm beginning to wonder why I'm doing the cooking."

Noah crawled off the bed, still laughing.

A moment later, she heard him slam the bathroom door.

She let out a breath. But Hunt didn't ease back from her now that Noah was gone. Oh no, instead, the naughty man slowly lowered his head and kissed her on the neck in a sensitive spot.

"This won't work," she said, arching her neck for ease,

because hello? Hot man kissing delicate skin. And the other morning had only added a few drops to the sexual well that had gone dry years ago.

"Oh, it's working," he said.

Was that some reference to the erection pressed between her thighs? "You're bad."

"I'd like to be. Thinking we should reevaluate the rules of our marriage." He ran his lips lightly along the skin of her throat.

Oh God. She'd married Hunt to protect Noah, but now she realized the danger in it—she'd also married the hottest man in town. No woman was that strong. "I can't, Hunt."

He lifted his head and stared down at her, a serious expression on his face. "I'll wait."

Her mouth twisted. That wasn't what she'd expected him to say. He knew as well as she that they toyed with danger by giving in to intimacy. "You seem awfully sure of yourself. We already agreed that getting too involved would be a bad idea."

"I agreed emotional involvement would be bad. But I'm thinking physical involvement will only benefit us both, as we figured out the other morning." He shot her a cocky grin.

She elbowed him lightly in the stomach on her way out of bed, and he choke-laughed.

Hunt lay on his back, both arms behind his head, smiling. "I'm here whenever you need me."

And that was the problem. She needed him too much.

CHAPTER TWENTY-THREE

Hunt looked around the kitchen he'd seen yesterday for the first time in over a decade and grimaced. What idiot thought it was a good idea to move back into this old place? He could kick himself right now. "Tear it all out," he said to Lewis.

Lewis brought out his measuring tape. "I'll give our designer measurements to reconfigure the kitchen, but otherwise, we can get started in a couple of days."

Hunt considered what else it would take to make the space livable, with all the sad memories it held. "I also want you to tear out the entry. The crown molding too. Might as well get rid of the flooring while you're at it. And I want all new interior doors." He spun in a slow circle. "Let's also knock out the walls between the kitchen and the dining room. The one between the kitchen and the living room as well. Too many damn walls in this place."

Lewis raised an eyebrow. "You said this was an update."

Hunt swallowed the sour taste in his mouth that had risen the moment he stepped inside. "I changed my mind. If

I'm going to stay under this roof, I need it to look like a different house."

"Why don't we knock it down?"

Hunt glanced over. "Can we do that?"

Lewis chuckled. "Hell, Hunt, I was kidding. This house must have cost a fortune to build, and it's in excellent shape. But don't worry. We'll switch everything out and it will look like a different place."

"You'll knock down the interior walls too?"

Lewis moved between the rooms. "I will if they're not load bearing. Let me get the guys up into the attic and the designer over. What style are you looking for?"

Hunt pondered that for a moment. "Something that won't clash with the exterior. Warm. The way Abby has her house set up."

"You want the designer to talk to your wife?"

Did he? His brothers might object, given Abby was brand new to the family and this was the house they'd grown up in... But they'd given him free rein, and Abby had a way of making a house a home. Even the crap-tastic cabin she and Noah rented. "Yeah. Have the designer meet with Abby. I'll go with whatever she picks."

"Smart man. Gen would approve." Lewis jotted down notes. "She really liked Abby, by the way, after meeting her at your wedding. Said you'd picked a good one."

Lewis was older and closer to his brothers' ages, but still a part of the pack they'd grown up in. And apparently Lewis's fiancée Gen had excellent taste, because Abby *was* a good one.

Abby was like no one Hunt had ever met. Beneath the scrubs and dark circles under her eyes was a beautiful woman. Frankly, Hunt thought she was hot in her scrubs too, and the dark circles were already fading now that she worked fewer hours. But all of that was on the surface. She was an incredible mom, funny, feisty, and—dammit—sexy as hell. She might not know it, but Abby was slowly killing him, sharing a room.

Hunt had had a taste of Abby on their wedding night, and now all he could think about were the soft sounds she made when he pleasured her, the smooth texture of her skin beneath his hands, and the look of joy on her face when she reached her peak. He wanted to make Abby come every day, all day long. But he held himself in check. Which meant he might burst.

Lying next to Abby at night and not being able to touch her? Torture. The sweetest torture. But he refused to make a move until she gave him the okay.

———

A WEEK WENT BY, and Hunt threw himself into the remodel. It was either that or throw himself over a cliff in sexual frustration.

This was good for him. He'd never denied himself the pleasure of women. It was character building, he reminded himself.

God, if his brothers only knew how long he'd gone without sex since meeting Abby. They thought he was living it up with his new wife. Little did they know that this was the longest dry spell Hunt had ever experienced.

Lewis and his crew of demolition animals got the kitchen and baths torn out, and the downstairs walls removed. One of the walls was load bearing, but Hunt wanted it out anyway. He agreed to pay a small fortune to have a giant support beam set into the ceiling, and it was worth it. The more the place changed, the less it reminded

Hunt of his childhood. Now if he could only get his temporary wife to welcome him into her bed figuratively.

Hunt might be going crazy. Not from abstinence—though that wasn't helping—but from lying beside a woman he craved more each day.

The more Hunt thought about Abby and their *arrangement*, the more he was convinced a physical relationship was the right way to go. Okay, fine, he was horny as hell, and his fake wife was incredibly beautiful. All she had to do was bend over to grab the plastic wrap from the bottom drawer, and he hardened. It was driving him mad.

Whenever Hunt had pictured a future with a woman, his mind had always drawn a blank. But for the first time, he wasn't afraid of a committed relationship, if it was with Abby. For Hunt, that was huge.

Had to be because of the lack of sex. Nothing else made sense.

He pulled out his phone and shot Abby a text message.

Hunt: What's for dinner?

He'd offered to bring home takeout from Club Tahoe a couple of times this week, but both times Abby had shot him down. She might grumble about the quantity of food he and Noah ate, but she didn't seem to mind cooking, even if she wouldn't admit it.

Abby: Noah just ate mac and cheese. You're flying solo. Maria and I are going out to listen to music.

Hunt: Who's watching Noah?

Abby: I was hoping my husband would ;)

Abby: But if you can't, I can call Noah's grandparents. Though I hate asking them for anything. Or I can stay home…

No way. First of all, if anyone needed personal time, it was Abby. Between school and her job, the woman worked more hours than anyone he knew. Hunt was happy she'd cut back after their wedding. Besides, a little space was probably for the best. The sexual tension in their house was intense. One more night of going to bed without touching her, and the roof might blow.

Hunt: I'll take care of Noah. Boys' night!

Abby sent him a heart emoji, and his chest puffed up.

The woman was easy to please. And looking after Noah was just plain fun. They'd eat junk food, which Abby would complain about, but it was *Boys' Night* and junk food was mandatory.

Hunt considered their food options as he pulled into the driveway of Abby's small cabin, and his home of the last week. Burgers and fries? Ice cream? There was that chocolate volcano cake at the resort Noah liked…

He walked up the steps and let himself in with the key Abby had given him a week ago. Noah was at the dining table building a tower with magnetic geometric shapes. "Hey, Noah. How was your day?"

"Great! Mom's letting you babysit me tonight." Noah bounced up and down in his seat.

Hunt smiled and set down his keys and wallet on the

kitchen counter. "I heard. Start thinking of a movie you want to watch."

He filled a glass of water and took a drink. Then several things happened at once: Noah began rattling off names of animated films, and Abby walked into the living room, looking down and adjusting the hem of her dress.

Hunt choked on his water, spitting it out in a spray.

Abby's long, light brown hair fell in soft waves past her shoulders, and she was wearing makeup, which took her from naturally beautiful to supermodel stunning.

What the hell was he thinking letting his wife go out on the town without him? She was going to get hit on left and right.

Noah bent over and laughed hysterically. "You spat out your water!"

He ran to his mom and wrapped his arms around her waist. "Mommy, you look pretty."

Abby smiled and kissed Noah's head. "Thank you, honey."

She looked up at Hunt, and her eyes widened.

What did she think she was doing going out looking like that? She was a married woman, for God's sake. Fine, it was a marriage in name only, but it didn't feel like that. It felt like she was *his*. And Hunt didn't share.

"Can I talk to you for a moment?" he said.

Abby was still staring at him uncertainly, but she nodded and turned to Noah. "Be good tonight, okay? Try not to eat too much of the bad food Hunt brings into the house."

Noah giggled.

Busted. And Hunt felt no shame. *Boys' Night.*

He touched Abby's elbow as she grabbed her purse, and

guided her out the front door, closing it so they couldn't be overheard. "Where are you going?"

Abby rummaged around in her purse, pulling out car keys. "I told you over text. I'm going to listen to music with Maria." She scrunched one eye. "I think we're going to some new brewery that showcases up-and-coming bands."

Hunt leaned a palm against the doorframe, his other hand on Abby's hip. "I don't like it."

She looked at his hand on her hip, and her brow furrowed. "You don't want to watch Noah? Because—"

"Not that part." He scanned her body heatedly, lingering on her hips and breasts beneath the fitted, stretchy black dress she wore. Black heels accentuated her toned legs for the icing on the cake. He wanted to lick every inch of her. "I don't trust single men around you." He thought about that for a moment. "Not the married ones, either."

Her mouth quirked. "Hunt, do you realize how ridiculous that sounds?"

"Like I'm being a possessive ass? Yes." He leaned forward and inhaled. "You smell too damn good too."

Abby held back a smile, but she leaned closer as well. "This is silly. I haven't dated a man since before Noah's father. Our fake wedding night was the most action I've gotten in ages."

He leaned the last few inches in and brushed her lips with his. "Damn straight. And there's more where that came from. I want you."

She sighed. "This is all your fault. I blame your biceps. And your chest. And your wandering hands. After we-we... Well, this week has been awkward. We never should have done what we did on our wedding night, because now that's all I can think about."

Finally, they were on the same page. "We want each

other. We're married. If you think about it, it's our job to procreate." He shot her a crooked grin.

She pointed a finger at him. "That's not true, and you know it. Sex between us will complicate things."

"Or make things *less* complicated. Nothing is more stressful than the sexual tension going on in this house. Think of fulfilling our needs as therapy. Because I assure you, you'll be thoroughly relaxed by the time I'm done."

She swallowed. "I'll think about it. After I go out with Maria. I gave up everything when I started dating Noah's father. I won't do that again."

"I'm not asking you to give up your friends. Just remember what's waiting for you at home." He kissed her, this time wrapping his arm around her small waist and dragging her to his chest, expressing with his mouth all the things he wanted to do with his body.

He set her gently aside, but she wobbled in her heels, staring at him in a daze. "Call me if you need a bodyguard," he said, his gaze skimming her. "In that dress, you'll wreak havoc on the male population in this town."

Then Hunt did what he wasn't sure he'd be able to do and watched Abby walk away.

CHAPTER TWENTY-FOUR

Damn Hunt and his kisses. How was Abby supposed to focus on having a good time when all she could think about was the way he'd made her body melt with only his mouth and tongue? Which had her thinking about other things he might be good at with his tongue...

Abby dropped her head in her hands.

"Everything okay?" Maria asked.

Abby looked up and smiled. "Yes, fine."

"Are you sure? Because I could have sworn you wouldn't agree to go out with me tonight, now that you have a hot new husband in your bed." She sent Abby an exaggerated wink.

Maria knew about her arrangement with Hunt, but apparently hope sprang eternal.

"Hunt was fine with it." Actually, that wasn't true. He hadn't seemed fine. But he'd let her go without an argument.

Hunt might be territorial, but he trusted her, and that combination was sexy as hell. Of course, he'd branded her with that hot kiss first, the devil, ensuring all she could think about was what would happen when she got home. And the more she thought about it, the more she considered taking him up on his offer.

Sex. With Hunt Cade, master of all sexual exploits.

But there was more to their connection, and that was the risky part. It wasn't purely physical—it never had been. He'd slowly revealed a giving, supportive guy beneath the sexy exterior. And he loved her son. Abby could easily fall in love with her husband, and that would be disastrous. By all accounts, Hunt Cade wasn't a relationship person.

A couple of hours later, after listening to music and conversation she'd struggled to focus on, Abby exited her car and walked up the driveway to her house. All appeared quiet, with the interior lights dimmed and the flicker of the television coming through the blinds. Hunt must still be awake.

She took a deep breath and opened the front door quietly, careful to not wake Noah in the other room, with the house the size of a shoebox.

But Abby didn't find Hunt waiting up, and Noah wasn't in his bed.

Hunt was sprawled asleep across the couch, one leg supporting his weight on the floor, his head tipped back against the couch arm. And Noah was splayed on top of him, mouth open, his back to Hunt's front. Hunt's arm lay across Noah's middle, protectively supporting her son even in sleep.

Abby breathed in and let out a controlled exhale. The breathing should have kept her calm, but tears welled to her eyes anyway. Noah cuddled up with Hunt was the closest thing she'd ever seen to her son with a father figure, and a light choking sound escaped her throat.

Hunt blinked his eyes open. Confusion filled his face,

and then his gaze landed on Abby. A dark, possessive look crossed his eyes before he glanced down, seemingly surprised to find Noah asleep on top of him.

In one smooth motion, Hunt stood and cradled Noah in his arms. He silently carried Noah to the back of the house.

Abby kicked off her shoes and went into the kitchen for a glass of water. She needed to clear her head. The adorable scene with Hunt and Noah would not dictate her decision to take things further with Hunt.

Fine, it was swaying her.

She'd never seen her son love a man the way he loved Hunt. And Abby couldn't blame Noah, because she was half in love with Hunt too.

Hunt returned to the living room rubbing his rumpled hair. "Everything okay?" He stretched his back and yawned.

Abby set her glass on the counter and walked over. "Noah asleep?"

"Passed out." He smiled abashedly. "I guess I passed out too. Sorry, didn't mean for Noah to fall asleep out here."

Abby didn't care that Noah had stayed up too late. Her son had been cared for and protected by a man who had no reason to love him the way he did.

She unzipped the back of her dress and watched as Hunt's eyes tracked her hands.

"Abby," he said low. "We don't have to do this. I mean, we can. I won't talk you out of it." He rubbed his jaw as she slid her dress past her waist and over her hips covered in black satin. The material pooled onto the floor. "But I don't want you to feel pressured."

Pressured? She was the luckiest woman alive to have Hunt look at her the way he did. He'd been staring at her body the entire time he spoke. But now he was looking into her eyes, and there was so much there she could read, and some things she couldn't. Lust, awe, and something deeper.

She stepped forward and pressed her body to his, dragging his head down for a kiss.

And that was all it took.

Hunt wrapped his arms around her waist and picked her up, drugging her with his lips and tongue. He walked into the bedroom and quietly closed the door, even now conscientious of the little boy in the other room.

He crossed the room and sank onto the bed, and Abby tumbled on top of him.

Hunt leaned to the side, and her back pressed into the mattress. "Still want to do this?" He ran his hand down her ribs and across her black satin bra, a finger brushing her nipple.

"If you stop now," she said, "I will kill you."

Hunt skimmed his mouth down her throat and gave her a masculine sound of approval. And then her bra disappeared and her panties slid off. She hadn't even registered him removing the bra until cool air hit her breasts.

Abby sat up. She might be fully naked, but Hunt was clothed. "Shirt off. Now." Not eloquent, but whatever. If they were doing this, she wasn't missing anything. She wanted to see Hunt in all his glory.

He reached back and pulled his shirt over his head while Abby fumbled with the fly of his jeans. Shaky fingers or not, she felt powerful and in control. This was *her* man. Maybe not forever, but for right now.

Hunt stood and shoved down his jeans and boxer briefs. He kicked them aside and slid back onto the bed next to Abby.

The lighting was dim, but enough filtered through the

window blinds to make her eyes bug out. No man was more beautifully built than Hunt.

She slowly ran her palm over his broad shoulders, across his chest, to tapered abs, taking in every sinewy edge and dip.

A smile turned the corner of his mouth, and his expression was indulgent. Until she wrapped her hand around his erection.

Hunt let out a sharp breath and tensed. "Abby, let's take this slow. It's been a while. I never go this long without..."

She looked into his eyes. "Is your reputation that accurate?"

He nodded, his gaze serious. "You can still back out."

Hunt was more than his player reputation. She'd never had cause to doubt his loyalty to her or Noah. "I'm not backing out. But we should use something."

"Always. I always use a condom," he said.

"Okay, then." Abby returned her hands to his body, back to where she'd left off. She wanted Hunt more than she'd ever wanted any man.

He rolled until he was on top of her and looked into her eyes. His gaze trailed down her chest and arms. "You're so beautiful that I don't know where to start. You're like a feast before a starved man."

She smiled, but then he covered her mouth and she wasn't smiling anymore. His tongue dipped, teasing her, and then he scooted down and licked her nipple, no foreplay with hands and fingers, just straight tongue on the pebbled peak of her breast.

Abby nearly sprang off the mattress, but Hunt held her down, his palm pressed lightly on her chest.

And then he was moving lower, his hand mapping her breast while his mouth kissed a path toward her belly. He lingered there and licked, trailing farther with his soft lips and tongue until he reached the crease of her leg.

Hunt lifted her knee, opening her to him, but she didn't have time to feel shy. He sucked along the crease between her sex and thigh, making her squirm.

He was so close...

His hand moved from one breast to the other, circling and plucking gently at her nipples while he intermittently kissed and sucked along the tender inside of her thigh. He skimmed his hand down her leg, reaching delicate spots behind her knee, and then back up again, teasing her.

Abby was about to say something to urge him along when he squeezed her nipple and pressed the flat of his tongue against her clitoris.

She arched and cried out.

He tsked. "We don't want to wake Noah. I have plans for you."

Oh the naughtiness, the implications... And how the hell was he touching so many erogenous zones at once?

Maybe his reputation *was* well deserved—not because of the quantity of women he seduced, but the quality with which he did it. She should care about the reasons he'd gotten so good, but at the moment, she really, really didn't.

Abby's eyes rolled into the back of her head. She could do nothing but take in the pleasure of Hunt's touch.

And then his tongue returned to the mother of all erogenous zones, licking and sucking and putting just enough pressure on that ball of nerves that seemed the center of the universe. She unabashedly writhed on the bed, moaning to keep from screaming.

She was going to come like she had last time. Hard and fast. And she couldn't find it within herself to be embarrassed. Not when she was mentally grasping for the release.

And then Hunt's mouth disappeared from her body and he sat up.

"What...?" was all she could get out before he turned her over onto her stomach. Hunt wrapped his arm around her waist and lifted her until she felt the warmth of his chest on her back. His thighs were between her knees, and his hand returned to her clitoris, wreaking havoc with his fingers.

He was doing it again, the multitasking. The sound of foil tearing came from behind, but his fingers never stopped working their magic, swirling around her clit and dipping inside her body. The next thing she knew, he was spreading her knees wider with his large thigh, one hand returning to her breast, the other torturing her in the best possible way with a clever finger on that bundle of nerves.

He entered her inch by inch.

Hunt Cade was well proportioned. Everywhere. She'd seen it, but now he was slowly moving inside her and she wanted to cry out. He felt perfect. Or maybe it was his warm skin and the erotic rhythm of his hands on her body. Whatever it was, he was drugging her. And bringing her to the brink before he'd fully seated himself inside her.

Abby bucked, and Hunt filled her the last inch. He didn't stop the slow torture of his hands once he was inside her. With her back to his chest, the two of them on their knees, he had access to every part of her body, and he used it.

Her neck arched back when the release came, and Hunt rode out her orgasm, not ceasing his steady rhythm until he'd drained every drop of pleasure from her.

Moments later, Abby went limp, unable to hold herself up.

Hunt eased her onto her belly and turned her over again

liked she weighed nothing. He plunged inside her, his eyes an intense blue holding hers. He lifted her knee and shifted his position until he hit a spot deep inside her that had her moaning and building up to another climax.

What the hell?

By the time her next orgasm came, Hunt was right there with her, kissing her lips, her neck, and moaning out his own release. The sound of his voice and his jerky, uncontrolled movements were sexy as hell as he let himself go.

Abby held on, even while her body convulsed, euphoria spreading through her.

She'd never let go—not as long as she had him.

Hunt collapsed on top of her, his arms supporting part of his weight as his breathing calmed.

After a few minutes, he lifted his head from where he'd tucked it against her shoulder and neck. A wicked look gleamed in his eyes. "That was fun. Ready for round two?"

CHAPTER TWENTY-FIVE

"**R**ound two?" she said, stunned. "I'm still recovering from round one. How are you conscious right now?"

Hunt rolled to his side, pulling Abby against him. "You inspire me," he murmured against her neck, tickling her.

"Or I'm the only willing woman in the vicinity," she said. "You promised to not be with anyone else. Not like you have options."

A queasy sensation rolled through Abby's stomach. Hunt had made it clear that this marriage was his way of helping her and nothing more. But now that she'd spent time with him and gotten to know him, she wasn't sure she wanted to let him go. She thought she could keep things casual. Now, she was pretty sure Hunt had ruined her for all other men.

She couldn't help her budding feelings for him even before the explosive sex.

Hunt tensed, and she feared he'd read her mind about wanting more.

"Everything okay?" she said.

"I don't want to be with you because you're the only woman around. You know that, right?"

Not really. "We're attracted to each other," she said hesitantly. Because there *was* sizzling chemistry between them.

"Attraction is putting it mildly." He shook his head and looked away. "I'm going to sound like a jerk, but you're the only woman I've ever been willing to commit to."

"But that was to help me and Noah," she said. He had agreed to a fake marriage, and Abby wasn't naive enough to believe Hunt's affection for her son hadn't played a huge part in it.

"Maybe. In the beginning. Now, I'm not so sure," he said.

Abby's face froze.

"What is it?" he asked.

"Nothing," she said, then smiled and kissed him. But inside, her heart and mind went into turmoil. She couldn't risk ruining their agreement for feelings built on shaky ground. What if Hunt panicked as the relationship grew, and he left her? She'd be back where she started, alone, and with Noah's grandparents breathing down her neck.

Since Abby's wedding to Hunt, Vivian had backed off, and it had been a huge weight lifted off Abby's shoulders. She couldn't risk losing the ground she'd made where Noah's grandparents were concerned. Not even for a chance at love.

She was a single mom, and if anything could force her to keep her feelings in check, it was her duty to Noah.

———

UNFORTUNATELY, over the next week Hunt tested Abby's determination to keep things casual at every turn. He followed through on his declaration of stamina, and *good God* did he prove himself.

As soon as Noah crashed for the evening, Abby and Hunt retreated to her bedroom and stayed up half the night putting Hunt's skills to the test. She was getting *so much more* out of this fake marriage than he was, she was sure of it.

Sex with Hunt was the best sex of her life. Though he didn't seem to be suffering.

Hunt had reached for her in the middle of the night last night. "Just one more time," he'd said, and she didn't think it was all about sex. He seemed to be holding on to her as hard as she wanted to hold on to him.

Abby leaned over the bed, blushing at the memory, and rummaged for a pair of leggings Hunt had removed. It was Saturday morning, and she heard Noah rustling around in his bedroom. Any minute, her son would come barging in.

Hunt slid his hand across her ass. "Mmm."

She slapped his hand away. "We just finished!"

He cocked his head. "Is there really such a thing as *all done* when it's so much fun?"

She leaned over and kissed him on the mouth. "You're awful."

"But does it turn you on?"

She giggled and reached for a T-shirt to hide the truth. Because, yes—yes it did.

Pretty much everything this man did was a huge turn-on. She only had to look at him these days before her mind wandered to where his hands had wandered a few hours earlier.

"To be continued later," he said, and waggled his

eyebrows. He pulled on boxer briefs and a pair of gym shorts and stood. "What do you think about Noah joining me at the house today?"

The "house," meaning the Cade mansion.

The house Hunt grew up in had to be at least ten thousand square feet. It was so far beyond anything Abby had known as a child that it might as well be in a different universe.

"Won't you be busy?" she said.

Hunt shrugged. "He can play in the yard."

"Oh, yes, *the yard*." Abby smiled. "Also known as the half-acre groomed garden that surrounds the mansion, complete with a two-story log cabin tree house."

"It's where I used to hide out. Can't blame Noah for his excellent taste."

"Are you sure, though?" she said, more serious. "He won't get in the way?"

Hunt wrapped his arms around her shoulders. "Noah's my bud. We'll hang. I won't be there long. Just need to check in on a few things. We're fortunate. Lewis had so many guys available after his project was postponed that we'll be moving in soon. I want to make sure everything's ready before we do. Besides, if I keep Noah occupied, my wife will be nice and rested when I get home." His voice took on a low rumble.

He was impossible. She couldn't say no to him when he talked to her in that deep, sexy voice. And yet she'd never be docile the way she had with Noah's father.

Abby had let Trevor call the shots in their relationship, believing his wealth and upbringing made him superior. But she'd been wrong. She nearly lost everything after Trevor died. Which was why she had immediately gone back to school at the local college as soon as Hunt moved in. She'd never be dependent on a man again.

Abby wanted a partner. Unfortunately, Hunt had become the perfect partner, asking for her opinion about the house remodel and deferring to her taste. He never dictated, and he loved on her like there was no tomorrow. What was she going to do?

"Why do I get the feeling you're giving me time alone for self-serving purposes?" she said, attempting to keep things light.

"Because I am?" He urged her close, her body flush with his.

Abby's eyes widened. "How are you hard after we just had sex?"

"I told you." He brushed a lock of hair off her cheek and ran his lips across her skin. "You inspire me."

"Only inspire?" she said, her thoughts drifting into brain-fog territory.

"I might like you a little." Hunt hesitated and pulled away, looking distracted.

A stupid flutter of excitement ran through her. It was too much to ask that Hunt's feelings for her had grown the way hers had for him. He'd already given her so much as it was. So she went for a teasing tone instead. "Just a little?"

"A lot." He sent her a look. "Abby, this is the first serious relationship I've had in a very long time."

Relationship. Not just an agreement. "And that's a bad thing?"

"I'm not sure. I don't have a good track record when it comes to loving women."

He might as well have poured cold water over her head. Which was why she needed to remember all she'd lost the last time she fell in love.

She didn't know if Noah's grandparents had a legal right to her son, but she wasn't risking it. Which was why she'd married Hunt to begin with. And she had to keep that focus.

Abby must have revealed some of her mental freak-out, because Hunt said, "I won't hurt you."

But it would hurt her when he left, regardless of if she kept her feelings locked down. She could lie to Hunt about how deeply her feelings ran, but she couldn't lie to herself.

Hunt had been the first person to truly care for her in ages, and now he was her lover. And she liked the way he smelled, even after his workouts. No man smelled good after workouts, but somehow Hunt did. When he slept, she cuddled up to him to get warm, and he didn't even jerk away at her cold feet. That was some keeper shit right there.

What was she going to do?

Hunt couldn't leave her, because she was falling in love with him.

CHAPTER TWENTY-SIX

A few days later, the Cade estate was ready to move into.

Levi, Adam, Bran, and Wes poured their long limbs out of their vehicles and scratched various body parts while yawning.

"You look hungover," Hunt said, eyeing one brother after the other. "What the hell have you been up to?"

Bran notched his eyebrow as if to say, "Really?" "We watched *Outlander* last night, and Ireland was feeling inspired after hearing the Scottish brogue. She kept me up late."

There were perks to living with a woman, and Hunt was feeling the effects of committed bliss too. For instance, he might have vaulted up the front steps a couple of nights ago to get to Abby before Noah came home. But a quickie wasn't really a quickie if all parties received full pleasure and still had time for a post-sex cuddle-chat.

Cuddle-chat? He was losing his mind. But what a way to go.

And then Hunt realized something else. For the first

time in as far back as he could remember, he was on the same wavelength as his brothers, with this whole committed bliss thing.

But there was a downside to committed bliss, which might have been why Hunt naturally avoided it. He grew more attached to Abby with each day that passed, and that had never happened. Ever.

Wes glared at them. "Not all of us stay up for fun times. I have a toddler. The only thing I've been up to is chasing my daughter around twenty-four seven."

"Feel free to bring her over if you and Kaylee need some time," Hunt said. "Harlow prefers me anyway."

Wes snorted. "No way. Kaylee told me about your brainwashing efforts to get Harlow to say your name." He pointed. "Stay away from my kid."

"So I'll pick her up tomorrow?" Hunt said.

Wes rolled his eyes. "Don't give her sweets. She hasn't been introduced to processed sugar yet. Knowing you, you'll use it to bribe her."

Excellent idea, Hunt thought.

He loved his niece. In fact, once his brother had had a kid, it got Hunt thinking about having a Harlow of his own. Until now, Hunt couldn't picture any woman he'd want to have a child with, but Abby was an amazing mother. And Hunt sure as hell enjoyed practicing baby-making with her.

Hunt never tired of Abby or felt like he needed space. If anything, Abby was too independent. Now that she had more time, she was determined to finish her nursing degree, which Hunt fully supported. Except when it pulled her out of bed early for classes. That part could kiss his ass—he wanted Abby to himself in the morning before little feet scampered into the room.

Hunt scratched his head while his brothers drained

strong-smelling coffee. They were here to help move Hunt and Abby's things into the Cade house now that the old place was near completion. The plan had been to sell it, but maybe a sale wasn't needed? The Cade estate was a little much for a three-person family, but then there was the baby idea...

Ever since Lewis and his team demoed the house, Hunt had envisioned him and Abby living where he'd grown up. That was shocking enough on its own. He'd never imagined moving back in to his father's home. But he'd been so excited to move in today that he'd woken early and finished packing the kitchen.

Truth be told, Abby was more organized and had done most of the packing, but she was busy today. She'd left for her classes, so Hunt dropped off Noah at Club Kids and called his brothers over.

Hunt couldn't explain how he'd fallen into domestic bliss, except that it had seemed inevitable from the very beginning. He'd said he wanted to help Abby with Noah. He'd said he had the means and could protect her from Noah's grandparents. All true. Only he'd also wanted Abby, even if he hadn't admitted it to himself until now.

Hunt was in deep. He tried to tell Abby the other day his feelings had grown, but he'd botched it.

They were married. Did he need to communicate such things? Seemed to him that as long as he didn't fuck things up, it was a done deal.

Wes looked around the small living room Hunt shared with Abby and Noah. "You sure you want to keep this stuff? Doesn't seem like it's worth the work to move it to the new place."

"The furniture Abby and the designer chose for the house hasn't come in yet. Abby said this would do for now.

You think I'm stupid enough to go against my wife's opinion?"

Bran and Wes glanced at each other and promptly picked up the couch, hauling it to the moving truck Hunt had rented. *Smart men.*

Hunt was wealthy. He could have hired people to do this shit, but he preferred torturing his brothers. It was how they bonded.

It took two hours to load and unload everything from Abby's house into a small square space in the living room of the Cade estate. Noah wanted to sleep in Hunt's old bed, so they'd donated Noah's old one and moved Abby's bed into the master suite upstairs.

Levi glanced around the remodeled first floor, moving from one room to the next. "It doesn't look the same."

"That's the point," Hunt said, following him.

Levi glanced back. "I thought the point was to fix it up and sell it? What's with the new furniture you mentioned?"

"The place needs to be staged. We bought essentials. Most of the rooms upstairs will be empty," Hunt said.

What he didn't mention to his brother was that he expected to live there with Abby for a while before they sold. Not only because his family already owned the place and it had kid-friendly grounds for Noah, but also because the Cade estate would serve nicely for prosperity purposes where Noah's grandparents were concerned. They hadn't bothered Abby since Hunt married her, but it never hurt to hammer the last nail in the coffin of their dreams of taking Noah from his mother.

"Just be happy Abby has excellent taste," Hunt said. "She and the designer did a great job. It'll look like a show-stopper once the cabinets and counters come in."

Lewis and his men had torn down walls and thrown up

drywall, texture, and paint. They'd also moved electrical and rerouted plumbing for the updated kitchen configuration. The only items left were the finishes, which meant it would soon be time to invite Noah's grandparents over to show just how established Abby and Noah were.

Levi and Hunt walked back to the living room, and irritation vibrated off Levi's stiff shoulders.

Hunt sighed. It had been too much to expect his brother to appreciate the work he'd put into the place. His other brothers appeared pleased with everything, but Hunt should have known he could never please Levi. Why he even tried, Hunt didn't know. Maybe he was still trying to make up for the past. But now he had bigger priorities. Abby and Noah came first.

Levi glanced at the small square of items they'd moved in. "It's not much, is it?"

"No," Hunt agreed.

Levi cocked his head. "It's deceptive when you think about it."

His brother must not have gotten enough caffeine. "What's deceptive?"

"Well," Levi said, and scratched his unshaven jaw. "The way I see it, Abby's got baggage, but you wouldn't know it by looking at her possessions."

What the fuck? "I don't like the way you're referring to my wife." Levi was unaware of Hunt and Abby's arrangement—all the more reason his brother shouldn't talk shit.

Levi turned to him. "You're not emotionally mature enough to be married to a woman with a child. Not only that, a child whose father died. You just don't have it in you."

Maybe it was residual childhood anger radiating off the walls of the house. Maybe it was the pressure Hunt felt to not let Abby down. Either way, for the last ten years, Levi had never stopped telling Hunt how disappointed he was, and Hunt was fed up. "One more word, and I'll kick your ass."

Levi turned to him. "You made a mistake marrying that woman."

Hunt hurled himself at Levi, wrapping one arm around his brother's neck in a chokehold.

Levi had about fifteen pounds on Hunt, due to an inch or two more in height, but Hunt was solid muscle. With his momentum, Levi didn't stand a chance. He went down. Hard.

Levi twisted and elbowed Hunt in the stomach. "Have you lost your mind?"

"I warned you," Hunt growled. "Tired of your shit."

Adam ran in the front door. "Not again." He groaned. "Is this going to be a regular thing? Because I thought you two got out your aggression at my engagement party." Adam tried to pull Hunt off Levi, but Hunt head-butted him, and he staggered back.

Hunt went for Levi again; this time, he punched his brother in the stomach and elbowed Levi's chin. Blood pooled on Levi's lip.

Adam jerked Hunt's shoulder back, and was on him again, jamming an elbow in Hunt's spine.

Hunt tried to wrench Adam off, but the next thing he knew, he was flat on the ground. Adam had kicked his legs out from under him.

"Hey, uptight yuppie," Hunt said. "Where are you learning these tricks in your three-piece suit?"

Adam wrestled with Hunt to keep him down, ignoring the jibe. "I'm sick as fuck of you two fighting."

Hunt dropped his head back and let out a sigh. Adam

was right. Hunt needed to stop letting Levi get to him. This stupid shit couldn't go on.

Adam let up his hold, and Hunt jerked to his feet. "I'm happy to put the past behind us," he said as he glared at Levi, "but I refuse to hear anymore shit-talking about Abby."

Wes and Bran stood nearby now, having heard the commotion. Their arms hung loose at their sides as though they were prepared to jump in if need be. "That was a low blow, Levi," Bran said.

Levi wiped a smudge of blood from his lip. "Wasn't shit-talking Abby. Was criticizing Hunt and his immaturity."

"Seems to me," Adam said, brushing off his jeans, "you've both behaved immaturely. Hunt's not a child you need to scold, Levi. He's a grown-ass man. If he makes mistakes, it's on him."

Hunt glared. "Thanks."

Just then, Abby sprinted in the front door, and all thoughts of his brothers disappeared. Because she looked stricken.

Hunt ran over. "What's wrong?"

"I was on my way over," she said, "and I got a call from Club Kids. There's some kind of trouble at the beach... Noah's in danger."

CHAPTER TWENTY-SEVEN

Abby sensed Hunt's palm on her lower back, and then he was urging her toward his car. "Why aren't any of you at the club?" she asked.

When she received the call from Club Tahoe, she'd been on her way to the Cade house to help Hunt with the move. She hadn't planned on finding all five of them there.

"My brothers were helping us move in. I didn't think it would take this long."

"But you were arguing when I walked up. I could hear the tension in your voices from outside."

He opened the passenger door and let her in, then jogged around the front of his Range Rover and hopped in the driver's side. He started the engine and peeled out of the driveway. "We always fight."

Abby closed her eyes. "I can't take this right now."

"Abby," Hunt said. "Forget about my brothers. What did Kaylee say over the phone?"

Abby's hands shook. "There was an accident, and they called the Coast Guard."

Hunt squeezed the steering wheel and stepped on the gas. "It's going to be okay."

When she didn't say anything, he grabbed her hand, forcing her to look at him. "I promise, Abby. It will be all right."

His gaze was so sincere, as though he could fix anything. But no matter Hunt's intentions, he wasn't superhuman. "You don't know that." She was crying now, tears streaming down her face. "Kaylee wouldn't tell me what happened over the phone. That has to be bad."

Hunt didn't respond, but his jaw tightened and he returned his hand to the steering wheel as he maneuvered the winding roads to the club.

Before long, he pulled up to Club Tahoe and what appeared to be a side entrance.

He jumped out of the car and ran for a door.

Abby quickly followed.

Using a security card, Hunt let her in, but as soon as they were through the gate, he ran for the beach—and the crowd that had gathered there.

"Oh my God," Abby said, her chest tightening. She couldn't breathe, but she ran after Hunt anyway, gasping.

Hunt appeared to read the situation faster than Abby, because he stripped off his shirt and ran full tilt toward the dock, his brothers, coming out of nowhere, close behind.

Abby ran up to Kaylee, who stood by the dock, her arms wrapped around the shoulders of one of the Club Kids children, worry written on her face. "What happened, Kaylee? Where's Noah?"

Kaylee said something low to the child, who took off to stand with the other children.

She grabbed Abby's hand. "One of the boats broke from the dock, and we can't find Noah. We think he's on it."

"What!" Abby searched the water. Hunt had gotten on a Jet Ski and was starting it up. "Where is the boat?"

Kaylee pointed to the old wooden boat headed at a fast clip toward a large outcropping of granite boulders down the shore.

Abby lurched forward. "No! I need to get to him!"

Kaylee wrapped strong arms around Abby, holding her back. "Help is on the way. If Noah is on that boat, he's going to need you safe when Hunt and the others return with him. You're no good to Noah if you've drowned trying to swim to him."

Abby closed her eyes. She'd give anything to keep her son safe. Had, in fact, given up everything within her power to put a roof over his head. And now she'd married Hunt for the same reason.

But Abby's connection to Hunt had also put Noah in danger, because she'd agreed to let Noah continue on at Club Kids against her best instincts. Or maybe her instincts had been driven by fear. In any case, her son's life was in danger, and it was all because of Club Tahoe. "I don't understand. How did Noah end up on the boat?"

"We don't know for sure that he's on it," Kaylee said. "One of the employees saw the boat leaving the dock, and questioned me about it. Hunt wasn't here, so it shouldn't have been out. But the keys are missing, and someone released it from the slip. We've radioed the boat, but no one is answering."

By the time Kaylee had finished her last sentence, Hunt was already flying across the water on the Jet Ski. His brothers were in a larger Club Tahoe speedboat behind him. It also looked like the Coast Guard had shown up and were getting close to the vessel.

"But how did you lose my son?"

Kaylee closed her eyes as though in pain. "He was with the other kids this morning; I saw him myself. One of the new Club Kids attendants was in charge—someone who's less familiar with the children—and he didn't realize Noah had gone missing. We noticed it at the same time the warning went up for the boat." Kaylee squeezed Abby's shoulders. "I have people searching for Noah. We'll find him. He's often cleaning the old woody with Hunt, and with the woody out...our biggest concern is that he's on the boat."

Abby had seen her son taking care of the woody when she'd been late to pick up Noah. "My son is five. He'd never take the boat out on his own."

Kaylee shook her head. "I promise you, Abby, I've got everyone searching for Noah. The police have been notified. We'll scour every inch of this place until we find him."

But it didn't take scouring the resort, because the Coast Guard radioed in that the boat had been boarded and they'd found Noah. They were on their way back now.

Moments later, Hunt climbed onto the dock with a crying Noah in his arms, and Abby ran to them.

"Mommy," Noah said, reaching for her.

She pulled Noah to her chest and held him tightly. She would strap him to her body and never let him get three inches from her person if she could. "Are you okay?"

Noah sniffled, his wet cheeks dampening her shirt. "I was stuck on the boat and it was going so fast."

"I know, honey. How did you get on the boat?"

Noah leaned back and looked at her. "I work on it with Hunt."

Abby glanced at the man in question, her face hot with fury.

Hunt didn't even try to mask his horror.

"I polished the side like Hunt taught me, and put the rags away at the helm." Her son sounded so proud of his "work." Then tears filled his eyes. "But it started moving when I tried to get off and I couldn't get back." He hid his face against her chest. "It was so scary."

"Shh," she said gently. "You're safe now."

Abby looked at Hunt, but he was storming off toward one of his brothers, waving his hands furiously.

Kaylee walked up. "Abby, I'm so sorry. We don't know exactly what happened, but after Hunt reached the boat, he said the throttle had been tied down. Someone had tampered with it. I'll get to the bottom of this, okay? Nothing is more important to me and the rest of the staff than keeping the kids safe."

"Is it, though?" Her son had been bullied at Club Tahoe, and now, after Hunt had hired more people to watch over the growing children's program, he'd nearly died in a boating accident.

"Again, I'm so sorry," Kaylee said, rubbing Noah's back. "Are you okay, Noah? You're not hurt?"

Without lifting his head, Noah shook it.

"I'm taking him home," Abby said.

"Of course. Please let me know if you or Noah need anything. I'll drive over myself."

"Thank you," Abby said, and glanced up to where Hunt stood with his arms crossed, head bent down. Levi was talking to him, and he didn't look happy. "Tell Hunt..."

God, what could she say to him? He'd just moved her and Noah out of her only home, so she couldn't take her son there. "Tell him I'll get a hold of him later."

Abby couldn't worry about Hunt right now. She also couldn't go to the house he'd intended for them to live in. It was a strange place for Noah, and Hunt wasn't even there.

Likely wouldn't be there for hours after what happened today. Hunt was responsible for the beach and boating at the club; his brothers would never let him leave before this thing was resolved.

No, Abby needed to take her son someplace safe and familiar.

She grabbed her phone as she carried an exhausted Noah out of the club, and sent in a request for an Uber. Then she put in a call to her friend.

"Maria?" Abby said. "Something's happened. Can Noah and I crash with you tonight?"

CHAPTER TWENTY-EIGHT

"I can't believe you let this happen." Levi was going off on Hunt, and Hunt couldn't disagree this time.

He was in shock. Horrified.

If anything had happened to Noah... Hunt wouldn't allow his mind to drift there.

The moment he'd caught sight of Noah on board the breakaway boat headed for the rocks, he'd raced alongside and flung himself off the Jet Ski. Hunt nearly fell into the water before he'd managed to climb over the side of the old woody and reach the steering wheel. He'd cut away from the rocks and pulled up on the throttle that had been tied down by a thin string, seconds before collision.

Heart pounding, Hunt picked up Noah, huddled in the corner of the boat, and held him tight until Hunt's heart stopped racing.

The Coast Guard tied up next to them, and Noah had been quiet the entire way back.

This was Hunt's fault. He'd encouraged Noah to learn about boating, believing he was doing something good for a lonely kid. But Hunt was the lonely one, and he'd only put Noah in danger.

When Abby walked away, Hunt didn't do anything to stop her. She'd been right to leave him. To protect her son. Because Hunt had barely saved Noah in time. Somehow, someway, he was responsible for this, and Noah and Abby deserved better.

Why had he ever believed he could rescue them?

He'd dreamed of being a protector, and when Abby came into his world, he'd thought he could help her and Noah. But Hunt wasn't the pirate savior he'd dreamed of being as a child. Not a husband able to care for his family, either. He was a fuck-up. Just like Levi always said.

"Back off, Levi," Wes growled. "There are others who watch the kids, my wife included. You heard what Hunt said about the throttle being tied down. And someone had to have unmoored the boat. This was no accident. Somebody did this."

"You don't know that," Levi said. "What if Hunt had left the keys in the ignition, and the kid climbed on board?"

Hunt glared at Levi. "I've never in my life left the keys in the ignition. We all got the same boat safety training, and I'm by far the most experienced in this group, given *it's what I do*."

But Levi heard none of that. "The club could be sued," he said. "If not by Hunt's wife, who has every right to take us to court, then by the parents of other children who could have been harmed too." He paced in front of the dock. "We should shut down the children's program."

"No," Emily and Kaylee said in unison.

Emily touched Levi's arm. "This program has been wonderful for the children. Listen to your brothers. Something wasn't right today. We need to look into it."

While Emily talked Levi down, Bran walked over. "Hey, you okay?"

"Levi's right," Hunt said. "I might not have left the keys in the ignition, but this was my fault. I'm in charge." Hunt wouldn't admit it to Levi, but he could admit it to Bran.

Bran chuckled darkly. "Levi's wrong fifty percent of the time. He just thinks he's right a hundred percent."

Hunt shook his head. "I fucked things up. Somehow, I don't know where exactly, I messed up."

Hadn't he always screwed things up? It was what he'd been told over and over by Levi. It was what he'd believed even before that, when their mother died to keep him alive. Deep down Hunt knew he was the problem.

"Hunt," Bran said more loudly when Hunt didn't respond the first time. "Levi has always been hardest on you, even before you hooked up with his high school sweetheart."

Hunt sent him a look. "Thanks for bringing up old baggage."

"The point is," Bran said, "he's the oldest and you were a toddler when Mom died. Dad was gone, and Levi took it upon himself to look out for all of us, especially you. He treated you like he was your father."

Hunt flinched. "Fucking-A, that's a horrible thought."

Bran grinned. "Isn't it? But it's the truth."

"Well, he needs to cut the cord. I'm nearly thirty, and he's managed to make me homicidal with his fatherly love."

"Which is why I'm saying this," Bran said. "You're not irresponsible—"

"No, he's right about that part."

"Hunt." Bran squeezed Hunt's shoulder. "Stop beating yourself up. You and Emily built a children's program and made it into one of the biggest kids' projects in town. You've quadrupled the lake activities for our resort, and you're married now, with a wife and boy who love you."

Bran was wrong. Abby hated him right now.

But Bran kept going. "You've also just single-handedly taken our shitty, stuck-in-the-eighties, ostentatious McMansion and made it fucking cozy."

"That was Abby. She picked the finishes."

"Most of the finishes aren't even in," Bran pointed out. "The house looks great because of you, you idiot. You're not the bad guy. And I think you know that, or you wouldn't have married Abby."

Wouldn't he have? He'd wanted Abby, and he'd been willing to do anything to have her. Fix her car, pay for her son to attend Club Kids, marry her... Only Hunt's head was so clouded right now that he couldn't figure out if that was love or selfishness.

He'd begun to think for the first time in his life that he'd finally found a woman he could be with long term. Only now he wondered if it was his selfish need to not be alone. Maybe what he felt wasn't love.

But it sure as hell hurt when he'd looked back and seen her walk away.

"Think, Hunt," Bran said, pulling him out of his cloud of self-doubt. "Did anything strange happen over the last few days?"

"Strange?"

"You said the boat was tampered with. Was there anyone out of the ordinary on the dock? Anyone who stood out?"

Hunt shot him a look. "We run a resort. Almost everyone is a stranger."

"Don't be an ass. You know what I'm talking about. Anyone who looked suspicious?"

Hunt was about to dismiss his brother's paranoia when a thought crossed his mind. "The new Club Kids attendants we hired...I don't know them that well."

"And?"

Hunt thought back to this morning and dropping Noah off at the program. "The new guy rubbed me wrong. Didn't say anything specific, but he's not..."

"Not what?"

"Peppy?" Hunt searched for words, but that was the only one that fit.

"Peppy," Bran said. "What are you talking about?"

His brothers were driving him batshit crazy today, and he had enough on his plate. "Peppy, you ass...bubbly... happy to be around kids."

Recognition dawned on Bran's face. "Okay, so let's start there. We interview the new hires. And the Club Kids employees. Maybe they know something."

———

BY THE TIME Hunt returned to the house after being grilled by his brothers and talking to the police, no one was there. He went to Abby's old place, the one they'd cleared out that morning, but the landlord had already changed the locks, and Abby's car wasn't in the driveway.

Hunt had failed to protect her son; of course she wasn't waiting at home for him. That didn't stop him from calling her.

Only Abby didn't answer. And she didn't answer the next day, either.

Hunt loomed the halls of the remodeled Cade estate like a ghost, walking around the workers in a daze. He had no idea where Abby had gone, and Noah wasn't at the kids' program. Hunt knew because he'd gone the last two days, looking for Noah and making sure the program was running okay.

Lewis set his clipboard on the new kitchen counter and glared at him. "I'm gonna have to ask you to leave."

"It's my house," Hunt said incredulously.

Lewis shook his head. "Don't care. You're driving the workers and me crazy with your moping. You'd think a guy who had an essentially brand-new house in under three weeks would be more excited."

Hunt hadn't filled Lewis in on the club drama or the losing-his-wife drama, and he wasn't about to now. "So you're kicking me out, just like that."

"Pretty much," Lewis said. "Go make yourself useful somewhere. You know, at your place of work or with your new wife. Where is she, by the way?"

"Busy," Hunt grumbled.

He looked around the kitchen, which was nearly complete and insanely beautiful. He wanted Abby to see it, but of course that wasn't possible. Why would she return to the husband who'd nearly gotten her son killed?

If it weren't for Hunt, Noah wouldn't have even been there the day the boat accident happened. Hunt had been the one to drop Noah off, out of his desire to rush his family into the new house. But who cared about a house if there was no family to make it a home?

Somehow, he had to make things right.

———

"DID YOU FIND ANYTHING?" Hunt asked Kaylee once he made it back to the club.

Kaylee closed her eyes. "You're never going to believe

this, but we think it's one of the new employees we hired for the kids' program. He hasn't shown, and he doesn't appear to live where he said he did. I also can't get a hold of the references he gave me."

Hunt's face turned hot and he felt like his head might explode. "You didn't check the references?"

Kaylee's mouth twisted in annoyance. "Of course I checked. But his references aren't answering the phone now, and one of the numbers isn't connected anymore. Everyone who works with the children has been finger-printed, and nothing's come up. Whoever this guy is, he's never been arrested."

"But you don't know it was him that released the boat and tied down the throttle. You're assuming."

"Well, yes," she said. "Except that Brin saw him on the boat that afternoon before it was unmoored."

Hunt ran stiff fingers through his hair. "So this is all circumstantial."

"Yes, Mr. Lawyer, but it's pretty damning. It would help if you could talk to Noah and see if he remembers anything."

"I can't," Hunt said, clenching his palm into a fist.

Kaylee's brow furrowed. "Is he okay?"

"I don't know. Abby won't return my calls."

"I thought you lived together."

"We did, but she hasn't come home." Hunt would not cry. He was a man. Real men didn't cry.

Fine, he'd cried a time or two, but not since he was a kid. Fuck, why did he feel like crying now?

Kaylee studied his face and her eyes widened. She stepped closer and gave him a side hug. "I'm sorry. Do you want me to try to get a hold of her?"

"No. Wait—yes. Find out if she and Noah are okay. I

don't even know if they have enough money. Or who's watching Noah when she's at work."

Kaylee smiled. "I got this. You go back and finish that house you're remodeling."

So this was what it had come down to. Hunt couldn't hold on to his wife; he needed his brother's wife to take things in hand.

He wanted to bash his skull into a wall. His only consolation was that Lewis was going to love it when he showed back up at the estate.

CHAPTER TWENTY-NINE

"Mom, you're squeezing me too tight," Noah said.

"Sorry." Abby loosened her hold.

She'd been clinging to Noah these last few days, reliving every moment she thought she'd lost him for good. Nothing in her life had been more terrifying.

Abby stood and clenched her hands. "Are you hungry, sweetie? Do you want anything to eat?"

Noah shook his head, distracted by the television. Abby had loosened the reins on his TV time while they stayed with Maria.

Maria and her roommate were at work, but they'd opened their door to Noah and Abby, and Abby couldn't imagine how she'd ever repay them. She'd been able to save money while she and Hunt lived together, and it was time to find a new place, because she couldn't continue living with Hunt. And she couldn't stay forever at Maria's.

Abby rubbed her eyes, holding back tears. Marrying Hunt had been a mistake. She'd been distracted by her feelings for him and hadn't thought things through.

Hunt was a good man, but he'd put her child in danger

with the boat training he'd given Noah. She wasn't sure what all happened at the club the other day, but she knew that if it weren't for Hunt and Noah's closeness, her son's life would not have been at risk.

Vivian would learn about the accident and use it against Abby. Then she'd accuse Abby of marrying a man who was reckless; Abby could see the arguments unfolding now. To remain married to Hunt was asking for trouble.

Abby knew it would come down to this, a choice between happiness or her son. She just hadn't expected it to come as a result of her marriage to Hunt. Or under such frightening circumstances.

A knot twisted in her stomach and she paced Maria's small kitchen.

Abby hadn't returned Hunt's phone calls. She didn't know what to tell him. She should end things officially. After all, they would have ended their marriage eventually, and now it was prudent. But something held her back. To make matters worse, Noah asked for Hunt constantly.

Abby was stalling, but every time she thought of leaving Hunt, her chest ached and tears threatened her eyes.

She missed sleeping next to him.

She missed talking to him about her day, and watching him with Noah.

Not being with Hunt felt worse than the obstacles she'd faced supporting her son on her own. As though nothing was worth it if she and Noah didn't have Hunt. But that couldn't be right, because her life was in more turmoil than before she'd married him.

A knock sounded at the door and Noah looked up. "Mom?"

"I've got it," she said. "Stay there."

Abby unlocked the deadbolt and opened the door a

crack. And saw Noah's grandparents on the other side. Vivian was assessing the apartment building with her nose turned down.

"Grandma!" Noah shouted, and ran to the door.

Abby opened the door wider, and Noah ran into his grandmother's arms.

"Abigail," Vivian said. "And Noah." Vivian hugged Noah and smiled broadly. "How's my favorite grandchild?"

Noah laughed. "I'm your only grandchild!"

"Oh, that's right," Vivian said.

If Vivian hadn't put Abby through so much after Trevor's death, she wondered if they could have had a good relationship. All things said, Noah's grandparents loved Noah and were far more attentive than *her* parents, who hadn't even met their grandchild.

"I brought you a gift," Vivian said to Noah, and handed him a box with a picture of trucks on it.

"Yay!" Noah shouted, and began tearing it open.

"Not here, darling," Vivian said. "Open it in the bedroom while your grandfather and I talk to your mother. Don't forget to close the door."

Shit. This didn't sound good.

Abby nodded at her son, who'd looked up for approval. Noah ran off and slammed the door behind him. She'd have to remind him about closing doors quietly. Later.

She walked toward the couch and sat, gesturing for Noah's grandparents to do the same. "Is everything okay?"

Vivian looked at her husband. "We heard about the accident at the resort where your husband works. Why didn't you tell us?"

Abby swallowed. "The workers called for help immediately, and everything turned out fine." Not *fine*. Abby would have nightmares of that afternoon for the rest of her life, but Noah was safe. That was all that mattered.

"We were told a worker in the children's program had lost our grandchild. That Noah had snuck off and climbed onto a boat and drove out into the lake. He could have been killed. Supposedly, your husband carelessly skipped work that day and they were short-staffed."

Abby couldn't imagine Kaylee, or any of the other Club Kids workers, saying that about Hunt, but obviously Vivian had a purpose for this visit. "It was an accident. In fact, Hunt was the one to rescue Noah. Noah loves the club and the time he spends there. I'm sure they'll put more policies in place so that it never happens again."

"They lost my grandchild, Abby. Your son."

Abby let out a breath. She knew Vivian would never give this one up. "No one is more aware of that than I am."

Vivian glanced at her husband then back at Abby. "Darling, I know we've had our disagreements, but hear me out. We'd like to help you."

Help her? They'd never offered to help. And the times she'd asked, they'd flaked and made things worse for Abby.

"We'd like to relieve you of the financial responsibilities you've faced since Trevor's passing. It's why you married that man, isn't it?"

Abby didn't answer. She was terrible at lying. Also, she wasn't so certain anymore of the reasons she'd married Hunt. She worried it had been for more than security and protection for Noah. She'd liked Hunt and wanted him for herself.

"Don't answer now," Vivian said. "Just listen. We'd like to cover all of Noah's expenses: private schools, clothing, food, his housing."

"I don't understand," Abby said. "You've never offered to help before."

Vivian pursed her mouth. "That was unkind of us. And once we heard our only grandchild could have seriously been harmed, we sat down and talked about how we could have prevented such a frightening situation. If Noah lived with us—"

"Lived with you?" Abby jumped up. "No."

Vivian stood, but her expression was kind. "We don't want to take Noah from you, Abby."

Abby threw up her hands. "But you want him to live with you. How is that any different?"

"You could visit as often as you like and have shared legal custody. But he would be in our physical custody."

Abby was about to object again, rudely, when Vivian put her hand on Abby's forearm. It took everything she had not to pull away. "I promise I'm not trying to take Noah," Vivian said. "I truly want to help. But it would be easier if he lived in our home. We have so much to offer him. The best education money can buy. Anything he needs."

She meant financially. Trevor's parents were loaded. They could give Noah a life Abby would never be able to provide. Not on her own. She'd always have to depend on someone else.

It had been a pipe dream to think she'd ever finish her degree and provide for her son. She'd always been in over her head.

God, was she seriously considering this?

When she thought about it, she couldn't help but wonder if she was being selfish, holding on to Noah, when his grandparents could offer him so much more. If Vivian wasn't lying, and Abby could visit Noah as often as she liked, this could be a way for Abby to make sure her son was well provided for and still be a part of his life. "I don't know."

Vivian smiled. "That's all we wanted. For you to think about it. Take your time." She walked toward the door, with her husband silent at her side.

Noah's grandfather sent Abby a kind smile.

"We'll be in touch," Vivian said, and walked out, her husband behind her.

Abby sank back onto the couch. Most of Noah's life, she'd felt like a failure of a mother. She should have pressured Trevor into putting together a will and trust so that Noah would be provided for. She should have insisted they marry. Anything would have been better than losing Trevor and risking her son's security.

But giving Noah up? Even if it was only physical custody, the thought had Abby curling into a ball.

She wasn't sure she could do it. But she also wasn't sure she could force Noah into the lifestyle she'd grown up in. Financially broke. Parents working day and night. Too much time alone.

Abby wanted better for her son.

———

CHAPTER THIRTY

Hunt finally tracked down the address of Abby's friend Maria, where Abby had been staying, and just in time. He was losing it, crawling the walls of his now-finished house, unable to sleep or eat, worried sick about Abby and Noah. He also feared he'd lost his family for good. Because Noah and Abby *were* his family.

Hunt and Abby weren't supposed to stay married. He wasn't supposed to love her, but somehow, along the way, he'd fallen for the sweet, sexy single mother of his favorite club kid. He almost wondered if it had happened the night he'd met her at the club, before he knew she was Noah's mom.

Abby wasn't like anyone else. She was strong and thoughtful, and she felt amazing in his arms. All he knew was that he wanted her in his life permanently. Hunt didn't want to live through another day without his family. That was why he was on his way to Maria's house to grovel and do whatever he had to do to get his wife and Noah back.

Abby had left him. She hadn't said as much, but she was gone, and he feared it was permanent. Now that he knew what truly happened the day of the boating accident, he'd been able to think clearly and not allow past failures to cloud his judgment. The accident hadn't been his fault, though he took some responsibility for anything that happened at the dock and beach. But he'd failed Abby in one other significant way.

He'd never told her how he felt. That he wanted more. That he was ready for more.

Hunt climbed the stairs to the second floor of the apartment building where Abby was living with Noah. He checked the door number given to him by Kaylee, who had tracked down Noah's grandparents and stealthily found out where Abby was staying, then knocked on the door.

Abby answered. Wearing her scrubs.

She looked incredible, and he wanted to pull her into his arms and sink his face in her hair. "Hey," he said instead.

"Hey." She looked past him. "How did you find me?"

"Noah's grandparents."

Her eyebrows pinched together. "They gave you my address?"

"Not exactly. Kaylee sort of got it out of them. Can I come in?"

"Oh, yes." She stepped back. "Sorry, I was just surprised to see you." Her gaze swept his body, and he felt it everywhere. *Goddamn.* "It's good to see you," she said.

Hunt forced himself to not reach for her hand. "It's good to see you too. Are you okay? Noah okay?"

"We're fine. Noah ran to the store with Maria. She's going to watch him while I put in an extra shift."

Hunt nodded. He didn't like that Abby was working more shifts again, but at least she and Noah were both safe. "Good, that's good. Abby—"

"Hunt," she said at the same time.

"You first," he said.

She walked into the small apartment living room and sat on the couch, gesturing for him to sit as well. "I'm sorry. I should have called you."

"It's fine. I know how upset you were with me."

She twisted her hands together. "I was. Until I realized it wasn't entirely your fault. I was wrong to put everything on you. Wrong to marry you."

He held up his hand. "Wait, you regret what we shared?"

Her mouth parted. "Well, not exactly. It's more that I feel like it was incredibly selfish of me to put the burden of caring for me and Noah on you."

"It's not a burden if I wanted it."

She shook her head, looking down. "You wanted to help us—"

"Nope. I fell in love with you."

Abby's head shot up. "What?"

"I love you. Love your fucking scrubs." He took in her body. When he returned his heated gaze to her face, she was blushing. "Love your clogs, and even your cold feet."

"You never said anything about my cold feet." She covered her face with her hand. "You should have told me it bothered you."

"Why would I do that?" he said. "I love your feet and everything else about you. The way you hold your son. The way you enter a room, shy and sweet. And I love the sounds you make when I'm inside you..."

Two fingers peeled away to reveal her eyes. And they were half-lidded. She was thinking of their bedroom and all the times they'd consummated their fake marriage.

"Our marriage might have started as a convenient arrangement—I wanted to impress my brothers, and you needed security—but I wanted you. And I fell in love with you once we married."

Her hand dropped. "You've lost your mind."

"Since you and Noah have been gone, yes. Ask our contractor, Lewis. He'll vouch for my insanity these last several days."

"Hunt." She sighed as though pained. "I want to be with you, but I can't risk it. The boating accident... And Vivian. She'll use the accident and anything else she can find against me. It will never end, even if we stay married."

"Vivian can't use the boat accident against you," Hunt said. "Someone set up the boat to release from the dock, and the police are looking into it. No one will believe it was your or my fault."

He rubbed his brow. "Abby, there's so much more to say, but trust me when I tell you that there's nothing Vivian has that could be used against you."

Hunt dropped to his knee, closing the distance between them. "Please come back. Not being with you and Noah is killing me. I'll get rid of all the boats, put security cameras everywhere to keep Noah safe—whatever you need. Just don't divorce me."

Abby blinked. "The boat Noah got caught on was released *intentionally*? And wait...boating is your favorite thing in the world. Why would you give that up?"

"You're my favorite thing in the world. And I'd give up whatever I needed to in order to be with you."

She took in his position on the floor on bended knee. "Are you...proposing to me?"

"Of course not," he said. "We're already married." He shot her a cocky grin and pulled her into his arms. "So what do you say?"

"I don't know what to say since we're already married," she said in a saucy tone.

He laughed and eased away so he could hold her hand. "Abigail Cade, will you marry me?"

She paused. Way too damn long for Hunt's sanity. And then she said, "I'm not sure things could get worse than they've been without you. Both Noah and I have been miserable." And then Abby's mouth turned into a smile that slowly lit up the corners of her eyes. "Yes, I'll marry you. Life is no good without you, Hunt Cade."

———

HUNT THOUGHT *he* was the most excited person to finally return with his family to the Cade estate—now his and Abby's home—but he was wrong.

Noah barely gave him a hug, before he was tearing through the house, touching all the shiny new appliances and paint on the walls. Marking them up, of course.

"Noah," Abby said. "No hands on the walls."

"I don't care," Hunt said, and pulled her into his arms. "This house will be a home where kids can live and make messes."

They heard Noah shouting and what sounded like him jumping up and down on one of the beds upstairs.

Abby momentarily glared at the ceiling. Then she glanced around. "It's so pretty. I can't believe how nice it turned out."

"You did a great job," he whispered, and kissed her neck. God, he'd missed the smell of her, the taste of her.

Waiting until she'd gotten off her shift to bring her here had been torture. She'd refused to call in sick, so he'd helped out Maria and taken Noah fishing.

"Maybe we should check out our bedroom," he murmured.

Abby sighed. "We can't. Noah's awake."

Hunt looked up, calculating. "What time does that kid go to bed?"

"In, like, four hours. Can you wait that long?" she said, chuckling.

"No."

"Hunt!"

"Fine," he said, and huffed out a mock sigh. "I can wait. Come on." He dragged her by the hand. "We might as well look around while you leave me pining."

The doorbell rang.

Abby looked to Hunt. "Are you expecting someone?"

"No one. I told my brothers to stay away."

She squeezed his hand. "That was naughty of you."

He laughed. "It was the smartest thing I've ever done. If I hadn't, they'd be over, harassing me and preventing things like this." He leaned forward and kissed her, ending it with a gentle nip at the corner of her mouth she was always worrying.

Hunt lifted his head, and Abby's eyes were glazed over.

"Okay, now *I'm* pining," she said.

"Good." He walked to the door. "We can get right to business as soon as Noah crashes."

Hunt opened the door, and an older man and Vivian stood on the stoop, their expressions pinched.

Wonderful, Hunt thought, and sighed. "Can I help you?" he asked Noah's grandmother.

"You're that man," Vivian exclaimed.

Hunt laughed. "I am a man, yes." He glanced at the person next to her. "I see you have one of your own."

"Don't be ridiculous," she said, and pushed her way in.

"Vivian?" Abby said. "Why are you here?"

"We had a deal," Vivian said. "Our grandchild would live with us."

Abby's eyes narrowed. "I said I would think about it."

Vivian straightened her back. "And have you decided?"

"Yes. Noah will stay with me. We'll live here, with my husband. This is our new home." Abby stretched her arms wide. "My husband and I can give Noah all the possessions and private education he needs. And love. He'll have more love than he knows what to do with."

Hunt walked over and wrapped his arm around Abby's waist. "Was there anything else you needed?"

Vivian pointed. "This man nearly got our grandchild killed, Abby. He's in charge of the boats, including the one that trapped Noah."

"What else were you told about that day?" Hunt asked.

Vivian scoffed. "Just that you were the one in charge, and people like that Donovan person, who cares for the children, aren't reliable. Abby put our grandchild in a dangerous situation, leaving him at your establishment, and we've notified Child Protective Services."

Hunt glanced around. "I don't see CPS here. I guess they're not worried."

"Now, see here—" Vivian began.

"No," Hunt said. "I don't think I will."

"Hunt?" Abby asked.

He looked down and squeezed her waist. "We didn't have time to go through all the details earlier, but I've been doing some digging while you were away. I found out a few things you should know." He looked at Noah's grandparents. "The first is that Trevor's parents hired an attendant to work at Club Kids. How else would they know his name? I never said it."

Abby looked at Vivian. "Is that true?"

Vivian blustered for a moment. "Don't trust anything this man says. I can't believe you moved back in with him. I had hoped that by moving in with your friend, you'd come to your senses."

"I hired a private investigator," Hunt said. "That's how the club tracked down this Donovan kid. Noah's grandparents hired him to get a job at Club Kids and make the place look unsafe.

"Donovan saw Noah wiping down the old boat that day," Hunt continued. "As soon as Noah boarded to put the rags away, Donovan cut the boat loose from the dock. He'd waited until I wasn't around, and rigged the throttle ahead of time. He's the person who nearly got your grandchild killed."

"No," Vivian said, her face turning pale. "That's impossible."

"Impossible that you hired him or impossible that he rigged it? Because we have his confession."

Vivian's mouth opened and closed. She glanced at her husband, who shared an equally worried expression. "We never told him to set a boat loose."

"But you hired him to work at Club Kids?" Hunt asked.

"Well, yes," she said pertly. "To keep an eye on Noah."

"And from what he confessed," Hunt said, "to make the place and his mother look negligent."

Vivian went silent. It was her husband, Noah's grandfather, who spoke up next. "We never would have agreed if we'd known harm could come to Noah or any of the children. Are you certain it was Donovan who did this?"

"He was caught in a lie and confessed to the whole thing," Hunt said. "Told the police he met you in church."

Noah's grandfather grabbed Vivian's elbow. "Come on, Viv. Let's leave them alone."

She pulled back. "No. He's wrong. Donovan would never have done that. It's this man who put Noah in danger."

Hunt stood straighter. "I'd protect Noah with my life."

The grandfather urged Vivian out. She followed, but she said over her shoulder, "You'll hear from our lawyers."

Hunt closed the door behind them, and Abby looked over, frightened. "Are you sure about this Donovan person?"

"He's facing charges after his confession. I'm certain."

"But Vivian and her lawyer..." Abby looked to where Noah's grandparents had departed.

"Don't worry about them. I've been in contact with our lawyers since before we married. They know everything. Noah's grandparents have no leg to stand on. Never did. They can't take Noah from you. And if you decide to press charges, it's possible for you to get a restraining order to prevent them from seeing Noah."

"No," she said. "It would hurt Noah, and I don't want him to lose the only part of his father he has left. They're not bad people, just terribly sad after losing their son. They changed after he died."

Hunt pulled her into his arms. "Then we won't. But I want you to know you never have to fear them again. And that I'm here for you."

She looked into his eyes. "I love you, Hunt Cade."

He smiled the widest smile she'd ever seen. "I love you, Abby Cade. And hey, look, you don't even need to change your name after our next wedding, since you did it the first time we married."

Abby grinned. "How did I catch such a sexy, smart husband?"

"It was the clogs."

Abby laughed. "If I thought those things would land me the hottest guy in town, I would have worn them more often."

"How many more hours until bedtime?" Hunt asked.

Abby looked down at her phone. "Three hours and fifteen minutes."

He sighed. "I guess I can wait that long."

"*Or*," Abby said, "we can put on a movie for Noah and sneak away."

Hunt's eyes turned half-lidded. "You're the smartest woman I've ever married. *Yes*. Right now." He picked her up and threw her over his shoulder, and she laughed.

"I'm the only woman you've married, you Neanderthal!" She smacked his ass as he climbed with her up the stairs.

"Neanderthal or not, I was smart enough to choose you. And for the record, I prefer *pirate*. I've got my booty and I don't plan on letting her go."

CHAPTER THIRTY-ONE

Abby turned on a movie for Noah, but her son was so chatty and excited that she and Hunt decided to join him and call in for takeout.

Hunt closed the door to their bedroom hours later. "Finally alone." He sent her a heated look.

She glanced around casually, as though he didn't affect her. "Is this the master?"

Hunt pulled off his shirt, and Abby's breath caught. "It can be," he said. "But there are four other bedrooms with bathrooms on this level. This isn't the largest, but it has the best view."

Abby looked out one of the windows onto the yard and the log cabin tree house. "So we can watch Noah play?"

"Yes. And our other children."

Abby choked. "Other children? As far as I know, I just have the one."

Hunt pulled her to him, shimmying off her top as he did. "I've been thinking we need one or two more. And I want to officially adopt Noah. With your approval."

Abby held up a finger. "We'll get to the one or two more

children in a moment. What do you mean you want to adopt Noah?"

He held her face. "I never want you to have to worry about anything, no matter what happens to me. I want to adopt Noah and set up a trust fund for him."

Tears filled her eyes. "You're the worst player on the planet."

His chin jerked back comically. "That's not what *she said.*"

"With bad nineties humor on top of it. Oh, Hunt, would you really do that for Noah?"

He kissed her. "I'd do it for you, and for me, and absolutely for Noah. I love that kid like a son."

She kissed him and slid her hands up his back. "I would love for you to adopt Noah."

He unfastened the snap on her jeans. "Now that that's settled, what about my other proposition?"

Her bra was off. When the hell did he remove it? He was doing that thing with his fingers on her nipples again. "Hmm? What proposition?"

"One or two babies."

That snapped Abby out of her lust haze. "We haven't even had our second wedding."

"Okay, so not right now. You'll probably want to finish nursing school first. Though I insist you take classes later in the day. Your morning classes are messing with our sex life."

She laughed. "Yes to the later classes. They were pretty brutal on me too."

"And the baby?"

Abby narrowed her eyes. "I'll think about it. Let's see what happens here first. I need to make sure we're doing it right."

He picked her up and tossed her on the bed. "Insolent wife. I'll show you how it's done."

Hunt pounced on her, and she tried to roll him over and get on top, but it was like moving a boulder.

Hunt lifted an eyebrow. "Yes? Did you want something?"

"Roll over, husband. I want to mount you."

Hunt's nostrils flared. "I love it when you talk dirty."

Hunt flipped over, and Abby crawled on top of him.

She looked around. "I like it up here. Makes me feel powerful." She ran her hands down Hunt's chest, circling his nipples the way he tortured hers.

Hunt folded his arms behind his head. "And I like a woman who knows what she wants."

He was so smug… Abby scooted lower and loosened the fly on his jeans.

Hunt breathed in unsteadily. "Feel free. I won't stop you."

Abby sent him a wicked look and trailed kisses down his chest. "No? Well, then I'll take advantage."

By the time Abby reached Hunt's lower stomach, all of his muscles had gone taut.

He cleared his throat. "Do you think you should take off the rest of your clothes?"

"Excuse me?" she said. "I'm in charge."

He held up his hand. "My bad. Continue."

"I will, thank you." She reached into his jeans and slid her hand down his shaft.

Hunt's head tipped back. "Shit."

"Yes?" she said. "Did you say something?"

"Nothing," he choked, as she swirled her thumb along the head of his erection.

Abby sat back farther and pulled off Hunt's jeans and boxer briefs. He stared down.

"You look worried, husband." She kissed his upper thigh.

"Worried?" he said distractedly. "No, no—just enjoying the view."

She grinned and licked his length from base to tip. "Me too."

Hunt groaned, eyes wide. "I can't." He sat up and hoisted her up his body. "Been too long. Need to be inside you. Good?"

She laughed. "Yes, caveman. We'll try this again when your upper brain is functioning and full sentences are coming out."

Hunt grunted and swirled his tongue around her nipple, moving his hand down her pants, fingers circling and dipping and hitting all the spots that were going to make her explode.

Hunt switched their positions, him on top, and stripped off her pants. He positioned his hips between her thighs. "Let the baby-making practice begin." And he plunged into her body.

Abby cried out at the fullness, the pleasure.

Hunt hiked her leg and hit her somewhere deep with his next thrust that had her head thrashing about. "Stay with me, woman, or this will be quick. If you start, I'll start—"

Too late.

Her orgasm hit, and she clung to Hunt. He followed her a second later, thrusting inside her and moaning out his release.

When his breathing calmed down, Hunt lifted his head. "Damn, that was too fast. Round two?"

EPILOGUE

At their second wedding, Hunt's bride wore pale pink. "You look beautiful," he said, and kissed his wife.

They'd just said their vows and walked down the narrow yacht aisle, and though Hunt's vows the first time around had been sincere, his vows the second time held more meaning.

Hunt and Abby were in it for life, and he couldn't be happier.

"Why thank you, husband," Abby said as she cradled her round tummy. "The baby kicked through the entire ceremony. I think it knew we were on a boat on the lake for the first time."

Hunt touched his wife's six-month-round belly. Abby had wanted to wait a year or two before they had a child, but nature and hormones took over. "Smart kid. Little does he know, we'll be spending a lot more time on the lake in the future. Like, for the rest of his life."

"Smile for the camera!" the wedding photographer said, and Abby and Hunt grinned, his arm protectively holding her waist.

Abby's mouth twisted. "These are my only wedding pictures, and I'm the size of a hot air balloon."

Hunt winced. "I forgot to hire a photographer for the first wedding. But just think, our son is in all of these pictures. He'll love that."

A spark lit her eyes. "You keep referring to the baby as a boy."

He leaned over and kissed her lips. "That's because I want a girl, but since my parents had all boys, I'm sure I'll be equally cursed."

"Cursed," she scoffed.

"Very generously cursed," he amended.

"What does that even mean?"

Married only a few minutes and he was already working his way into the doghouse. "You've seen how me and my brothers are together."

"Loving, yes, I've seen."

Hunt gave her a look. "Not exactly how I'd characterize my relationship with my brothers, but okay. Anyway, if you and I have a son, the genetics are not in our favor. I'm not sure your beauty and brains could outmatch male Cade sperm and their need for dominance."

"Your brother had a girl," she pointed out.

"Yeah." He rubbed his chin. "That was an odd occurrence. I'm sure it won't happen again."

The photographer set up to take another picture, and Hunt turned them in that direction.

"Well," she said, "you'd be wrong. We're having a girl."

Hunt's jaw dropped and he stared at his smiling wife beside him. *Snap. Snap. Snap.* The photographer caught the moment.

"What?" he said.

"Did you not wonder about the color of my dress?"

He glanced down. "It's pink. I thought you were going for the second-marriage-off-white color thing."

"Yes, but pink?" Her eyes twinkled.

"But...how?"

Abby waved to their guests across the yacht they'd rented for the wedding. They'd told everyone it was a second celebration of their love. The guests were also waiting for them to hurry up and finish taking pictures. "I imagine it was one of the hundreds of times you woke me in the middle of the night or in the morning before Noah woke or after Noah went to bed to—"

"I got it," he said, laughing. His boys could swim, and he couldn't be more proud of his powerful, manly sperm. Especially his baby-girl sperm. "But when did you find out?"

"Oh, about a month ago."

"A month! You've known for an entire month and you didn't tell me?"

"I wanted to wait until the perfect time." She looked around. "Now was the perfect time. Do you want to do the honors and share our happy news?"

Hunt sucked in a shaky breath. A girl. They were having a girl. He blinked back tears and kissed his wife. Passionately. He lifted his head and looked down at her beautiful face. "I love you."

"I love you, Hunt Cade, man of many talents."

Hunt turned to the crowd of friends and family, including all of Noah's grandparents—even Abby's parents, who Hunt had flown out.

He raised his fist into the air. "It's a girl!"

The guests cheered, and Hunt's brothers came over and slapped him on the back.

"Welcome to the club," Wes said.

Levi approached and stood awkwardly for a moment. And then his brother did the strangest thing Hunt had ever seen. Levi stepped away from Emily and hugged Hunt. "Congratulations."

Fuck. If Hunt wasn't already choked up about the baby-girl news, he was seriously holding back tears now. "Thank you."

"I was worried," Levi said. "Looks like I never needed to." He glanced past Hunt to Abby. "You take great care of your wife, Hunt. You'll make a great father too."

Hunt realized something just then. Levi ranted when he was most frightened or stressed. His temper, the way he'd talked to Hunt—all these years, it had been over fear.

Huh. That explained a lot.

Hunt couldn't wait until Levi and Emily had a kid. Levi would lose his shit the first time the baby had a fever or fell, or came to any harm whatsoever.

Emily hugged Hunt, and she and Abby made plans to get together in a few weeks, and then Noah's grandparents approached.

"We're so happy to have another baby in the family," Vivian said, Noah's grandfather smiling at her side.

It hadn't taken a lawyer for Noah's grandparents to come around. More like a few days of mulling over their actions, and how they'd put their grandchild in danger with their stupid antics. They'd eventually returned to apologize and make amends.

At first, Abby was leery, but over the last few months, Vivian and her husband had come over to the Cade estate— now named "Noah's Castle"—and spent time with Abby, Hunt, and Noah as a family. Noah's grandparents were even in treatment with a therapist to deal with the loss of their son. They'd asked for forgiveness, and Hunt's wife, being the generous spirit she was, immediately gave it to them.

What had come as a shock was how excited Noah's grandparents were when Abby and Hunt announced they were having a baby. It seemed Vivian considered this child to be her grandchild too, and that suited Hunt and Abby fine.

Hunt's parents were gone, and Abby's parents refused to leave their trailer for more than a long weekend. Noah's grandparents were a part of their lives, seemingly for the better, and there was never too much love to give a kid.

Hunt counted himself blessed a million times over.

He was mingling with the guests, shoving food into his mouth, and tracking his very pregnant wife, when Esther walked up.

"Dear boy," she said, and gave Hunt a big hug. She held his arms and leaned back. "I'm so happy for you. I just knew the right woman would tame you some day."

Interesting. Hunt never imagined he'd find a woman he would be able to love and hold on to at the same time. "How did you know?"

Esther smiled warmly. "Call it surrogate mother's intuition. Something seemed off when I attended your first wedding to Abby, but this one is the real thing." She held out an envelope. "This is for you."

Leave it to Esther to suss out the truth. "Thank you, Esther. And thank you for being here at my second marriage to Abby." He winked.

"I'm always here for you boys. You're the children I never had."

A man walked up to Esther and touched the small of

her back. He reached out and shook Hunt's hand. "Congratulations. Your bride is lovely. Lucky man."

"Indeed," Hunt said.

"More champagne?" the man asked Esther.

She nodded, and he walked off, hand tucked into sleek gray suit pants the color of his hair.

When he was far enough away, Hunt notched his chin in the man's direction. "So who's the new man?"

Esther swatted his arm. "Lenard is a friend, and don't you start nosing into my business."

Hunt held up his hands. "I thought it went both ways."

"No," she said. "Not with your surrogate mother. My romantic life is mine alone."

Hunt had always wondered if Esther and his father had a thing going on in his father's later years. Neither had said or done anything to indicate that kind of relationship, but the way Esther had looked out for them like a mother...it seemed possible there had been some kind of understanding.

Then again, his father never got over Hunt's mother, so who knew? He'd never know, given how open Esther was being. "Fine. Keep your secrets. For the record, he seems like a pretty dapper dude."

Esther looked over her shoulder, and Hunt would swear she was checking out Lenard's ass. "He is, isn't he?"

Good God. Hunt mentally cringed. "Right," he said. "I better go find my bride."

"Do that," Esther said. "And read the letter with her after you do."

Hunt made his way across the deck, greeting guests and tracking down his wife. He finally found her coming up from the restroom. His wife had to pee every hour these days, so it was a safe bet to find her there.

He hooked his arm around her waist and pulled her to his chest before she could round the corner and return to the guests. "There you are."

"Hunt, we need to return to the party," she said, but she was smiling and snuggling into his chest, her tummy a warm, round ball between them.

"In a minute," he said, and kissed her. Then he ran his hands down her sides and cupped her bottom.

"Hunt," she said in warning. "We have a very nice honeymoon/babymoon set up. There's plenty of time for that." She stood on her tiptoes and looked over his shoulder. "The guests are waiting for us."

"Esther gave me a letter and said I should read it with you."

Abby glanced down at the white envelope he pulled out.

Hunt blinked. "Actually, I think it's from...my father? That's weird. My name on the envelope is in his handwriting."

He opened the envelope and unfolded the letter, and Abby leaned on his arm to read along.

Dear Hunt,

Before you were born, your mother wanted a girl, but I wanted another boy. You probably never knew that, did you?

Out of all my sons, you got the short end of the stick. You weren't able to experience enough of the love your mother had for you boys. I thought losing her was the worst thing to ever happen to me. Turns out, my decisions later in life caused me my biggest regrets, and the ones I'll never forgive myself for.

I'm sorry I wasn't there for you and your brothers. In my head, you boys were my world. I thought I showed it by making a success of the club and providing for you. Turns out, being a successful businessman does not a good father make. I managed to push you away. I know that now. And believe me, I've beaten myself up over it.

Don't ever think you weren't wanted. Don't ever feel shame or blame for your mother's illness. She wouldn't have given you up for anything in the world, and neither would I. Not even to have more time with your mom.

I see her in you the most. You have her smile and her eyes, but what really hit me as you grew older was the way you both embrace life with both hands. You are one of five blessings your mother and I dreamed of together, and I hope someday you'll realize the same joy we did.

Only try to be more present than your dear old dad.

Oh, and one last thing: don't let Levi bully you. He carried you around like you were his son when he was in elementary school. Was cute back then. Not so much once you hit high school. That boy thinks he knows it all. Takes after his pops in that way. He genuinely loves you, but he's as clueless as the rest of us.

Trust your instincts. You've always been a good man, and I have no doubt you'll make the right choices in life.

I love you,

Dad

Hunt looked up, eyes watering for real this time. "Damn."

"Oh, Hunt," Abby said, and hugged him tightly. "That's a beautiful letter. And what a special time for Esther to share it with you."

Hunt wiped his eyes, and Abby kissed his cheek. "Sort of makes me wonder if my brothers received letters too. You know, after they married or fell in love."

"I don't know," Abby said. "You should ask them."

Hunt nodded and slowly took in a few breaths.

He looked down at Abby and smiled. "I'm the luckiest guy alive. I have a son, a baby girl on the way, and the most incredible wife a man could ever ask for."

Abby beamed. And then her smile fell. "Except I'm huge."

"Huge with our beautiful girl growing inside you. And I'm going to show you tonight just how hot I think you are."

Abby's face turned bright red. "You realize my hormones are raging in this second trimester. We'd better get home soon."

"You don't need to tell me twice." Hunt thought of carrying her through the crowd, then reconsidered. He didn't want to risk his wife getting jostled in her condition. He settled for holding her firmly at his side, and urging them through more guest greetings and toasts.

It seemed like forever before they made it home for the night, with Noah at a sleepover at his cousin Harlow's house. Hunt and Abby didn't leave for their trip until tomorrow, so they had one night at home together.

They sat on the carpet cross-legged in their bedroom, and Hunt held up a glass of champagne. "I love you, Abby Cade. Thank you for giving me the best family I could ever hope for. One I never thought I'd have, but always dreamed of."

Abby teared up and raised her glass of sparkling apple cider. "Thank you for standing up for Noah and me. For loving me. And for *loving me*." She winked.

Hunt raised his eyebrows. That was an invitation if ever he'd heard one.

Abby leaned over to kiss him, and he took advantage of her sketchy equilibrium and gently tipped her to the floor.

Abby laughed. "You're bad."

"And don't you forget it."

They didn't make it to the bed until much later.

———

Dear Reader,

I hope you enjoyed the final book in the Cade Brothers series, *Reforming Hunt*!

Have you read the Never Date series? It's the five books that come before the Cade Brothers, and feature characters like Jaeger & Cali and Lewis & Gen you met in *Reforming Hunt*. Be sure to check out the first book in the series ***Never Date Your Brother's Best Friend***. Like all my titles, the Never Date series can be read as standalone stories.

Scan the Linktree QR code below to access all my books and social media, or keep scrolling to the "Also By" page and click on your next great read!

xoxo,

Jules

ACKNOWLEDGMENTS

Any author will tell you that finishing a series is bittersweet. I'm going to miss these Cade brothers. I loved watching the affection they had for one another come to life in each of their stories. And, of course, watching them fall for the women who made them laugh, love, and find home.

The dad's letter at the end of each book was something that came up in book one, *Tempting Levi*, and once it was there, it had to be in all of the stories. In a way, the father's letter was the closure the brothers needed to make a fresh start with the women they loved, and also to show a side of their father they'd not seen in life. Because sometimes men don't show their feelings. Imagine that!

As a writer, I stay in my lane, because I know where my skills are, so I want to give a huge thank-you to the people whose lanes I suck at and who take care of me. Gel from Tempting Illustrations, who makes beautiful graphics, Najla for her work on the covers, my editors Arran, Martha, and Chris, and Susannah Jones and Zachary Webber, the narrators of the Cade Brothers audiobooks who brought the characters voices to life.

I'm so blessed to create stories for a living, and it's all because of readers. Thank you for sharing the journey with me every time you open one of my books.

ALSO BY JULES BARNARD

All's Fair

Landlord Wars

Roommate Wars

Never Date Series

Never Date Your Brother's Best Friend (Book 1)

Never Date A Player (Book 2)

Never Date Your Ex (Book 3)

Never Date Your Best Friend (Book 4)

Never Date Your Enemy (Book 5)

Cade Brothers Series

Tempting Levi (Book 1)

Daring Wes (Book 2)

Seducing Bran (Book 3)

Reforming Hunt (Book 4)

ABOUT THE AUTHOR

Jules Barnard is a *USA Today* bestselling author of romantic comedy and romantic fantasy. Her romantic comedies include the All's Fair, Never Date, and Cade Brothers series. She also writes romantic fantasy under J. Barnard in the Halven Rising series *Library Journal* calls "...an exciting new fantasy adventure." Whether she's writing about steamy men in Lake Tahoe or a Fae world embedded in a college campus, Jules spins addictive stories filled with heart and humor.

When she isn't in her sweatpants writing and rewarding herself with chocolate, Jules spends her time with her husband and two children in their small hometown in the Pacific Northwest. She credits herself with the ability to read while running on the treadmill or burning dinner.

www.julesbarnardbooks.com

www.ingramcontent.com/pod-product-compliance
Lightning Source LLC
Chambersburg PA
CBHW061523310726

48972CB00008B/2304